FURROW AND SLICE

Richard Snodgrass

The Farmland Stories

with an Afterword by
Brian Taylor

Calling Crow Press

Pittsburgh

Also by Richard Snodgrass

A Book of Days

The Pattern Maker

Holding On

Across the River

All Fall Down

Some Rise

The Building

There's Something in the Back Yard

An Uncommon Field: The Flight 93
Temporary Memorial

Kitchen Things: An Album of Vintage Utensils
and Farm-Kitchen Recipes

Published by Calling Crow Press
Pittsburgh, Pennsylvania

Book design by Book Design Templates, LLC
Cover design by Jack Ritchie

Printed in the United States of America
ISBN 978-0-9997700-4-7
Library of Congress catalog control number: 2019904463

*For Chip, Jo Ann, and Adam
and, of course, as with everything,
for Marty*

A *furrow* is the shallow V-shaped trench that the share, or blade, of a plow cuts into the earth; the *slice* is the ribbon of earth that the curved moldboard on top of the blade lifts up and rolls over into the furrow from the previous pass down the field.

Giving up's the easy part.

PART ONE

THE STORIES

IN PASSING

The dirt road wasn't meant for two vehicles abreast, so each driver rode a little into the grass where the shoulder should be and came to a stop alongside the other driver's window and nodded.

"Thought it was time to check the fences along here," Walt said. "Don't want any of them to get the notion to start wandering around without me."

Albert nodded. "They told me at the dealership to let you know that pinion gear you ordered come in."

"You could've brought it with you. You could've paid for it too."

"That's why I didn't bring it."

Each man looked out the windshield in front of him, considered something, then looked back. "Did that heifer of yours get back on its feet?"

Albert nodded. "The vet came and gave it a shot. I thought sure she was down for good but. Time was a cow was down, she was down."

Walt nodded. "I'm going to slaughter a pig this weekend. You want some?"

"Sure. I'll take a side, if you can spare it."

"You want to help? I'm getting too old for hoisting 'em up myself."

"I would but." Albert pushed his straw hat up his forehead with a single finger, draped his forearm over the rim of the steering wheel like he was pointing the way. "Oh, they took Charlie back into the hospital. Started bleeding from his rectum."

"Take him into Pittsburgh?"

"Nope. Just over to Furnass. Onagona Memorial."

Both men, without thinking, looked over the rolling farmland to the clouds of smoke and steam rising from a cut in the hills a few miles away, from the mills in the town along the river.

"They say it don't look good," Albert continued.

"Wouldn't think so. When was this?"

"This morning. He's still conscious, they said, but don't think it'll take long. I was going over to see Margaret, after I came to tell you."

"Obliged. Let me know if she needs something."

Albert nodded, put the truck into gear, and rolled on past the other.

Walt sat a moment where he was, thinking of Charlie. Thinking of Albert. Bastard. He could have saved him a trip and brought that gear. Probably afraid Walt wouldn't pay him for it, and of course he would. He wondered if the other really came by to tell him about Charlie. Bastard. Well, no matter. There wasn't any sense in trying to see Charlie now, even if he was still aware. He put his truck in gear and continued to check his fences.

THE WEB

The web extended from the chain of the porch swing to the stalks of sunflowers beyond the railing. An enormous thing. Beautiful in its way, Miriam supposed, especially with the strands pearled with morning dew. It was that time of year again, the end of summer, the coming of fall, winter, a garden spider always built a web there, she wondered why they came to the same spot, could it be hereditary? This one the size of a half dollar, orange, hanging tail over teakettle at dead center. The webs kept her from sitting on the swing in the middle of the night, when she was awake from the heat or the hot flashes or who knows why. Not that she was afraid of spiders, in a lifetime spent on farms she had experienced a lot worse than a spider's web on her face, but still.

She leaned closer; the spider shifted, raised and lowered a leg in her direction. Was it aware that she was there? Could it see her? She had never considered such a thing before. She might kill it but she didn't want to scare it unnecessarily. Its apparent uneasiness with her presence got her thinking. Was there someone, something, watching her in a similar way? So large that her perception couldn't grasp it, though there were inklings? Well, she supposed that's what God was. Made sense. Able to crush us at any time.

Through the web she could see her husband on the tractor, mowing on a distant slope. The machine moved slowly among the strands like a green bug. Or like another spider, that was more like it. Tom reached the end of the row and came back toward her, down the web. By chance was he looking at the house at this moment? Looking at her unknowingly as she was looking at him? At this distance she couldn't tell. As he bumped along did he think about what he said to her? The way he said it? After what seemed a lifetime on this farm with him, she knew that answer well enough. She could be standing right in front of him, that wouldn't change a thing. Regret wasn't in his nature. He had never been concerned for her feelings, her reaction to things he said. Why would he start now?

The spider shifted again slightly, a ripple of legs. In the distance, Tom reached the end of the row and turned from her again. She raised the broom to clear away the web, then decided to leave it alone.

THE HILL LOVERS

" A re you sure he can't see us up here?"

"I don't care if he does."

"I don't want him to come along this road and find us."

He looked at her upturned face, and for a moment forgot his concerns, couldn't resist, kissed her. Then rested his cheek against hers, smelling her skin, her hair, trying to take her all in so he could call her back to his senses when she was gone from him. Again. He had parked his pickup here among the trees, on the road above her place, to be with her just a few moments longer, before he had to return her again to her world. Watch her walk away, into another man's house. Before he would start the wait again until they could think of some reason to see each other again. The wait to be with her again. The thought of not being with her now made his breath catch in his chest.

"He's cutting this time of year. Maybe I can tell him I asked you to take me into the market again next week."

"I can't go on pretending I'm just a good friend. His friend."

"That's why I think we should just tell him."

He listened. Among the wind moving gently through the clump of trees, the call of a mockingbird, a bee buzzing close to the window and away, he could hear the pull of the tractor, working the acres over the hill from the house. He drew her to him again and kissed her again, enveloped again in her smells and her promise and her softness.

"Do you love me?"

"Of course I love you," he said to her. Searching her eyes.

"Then love will find a way."

A line from one of her favorite songs. But he knew better. It was up to him to find a way. And he realized something else too. That whatever happened, it would be the three of them now, locked in an irrevocable dance. That to take her away from her husband would only draw the other tighter into their circle. The subject of endless talks and considerations and adjustments. Endless guilts. And, all things considered, he didn't know if it was worth it.

THERE GOES LOVE

"You know this ain't personal, or anything like that," Big Mac said. "It's like, you know, business."

"Yeah. Right. Business," Tom said.

The two men stood in the gravel lot of the diner. Tom had caught Big Mac as the other was about to climb into his pickup.

"So how's the farm doing this year?" Big Mac said, leaning on the open cab door. "You still running Angus?"

"I got some whiteface this year too. I'll make it okay. It'll be tight, but I'll make it. Though I sure could use the extra income."

"Yeah, I can relate to that, brother," Big Mac said as if he shared the same problems. Even though Tom knew for a fact from the guys at the feed mill that Big Mac's farm was thriving, that his construction business on the side had more work than he knew what to do with.

"I figured you'd be here about this time," Tom said, nodding to the diner.

Big Mac laughed a little, not all that amused. "You know me and the groceries. Got to start the workday right." He patted his potbelly to make his point.

Tom was digging a little hole for himself in the dirt and gravel of the parking lot, exactly the size and shape of the toe of his right work boot.

"I thought you got that new job over near Brown's. The McMansion for that pilot."

"Yeah. We started it already. It's just that I don't need any more help right now."

Out of the diner came Ben, Big Mac's brother-in-law. He nodded to Tom, said to Big Mac, "I'll see you over there." Got in his pickup and drove out of the lot. Spraying a little gravel as he made the highway.

"I had to," Big Mac said. "You know how it is, Brenda. . . ."

"Yeah," Tom said. At the crossroads a Lexus SUV stopped at the stop sign, then made the turn onto the main road. A young woman was driving. Dark hair, in a kind of bob, the points curled forward. An expensive gray blazer. For the briefest moment Tom wondered what it would be like to be with a beautiful woman like that. Then thought. That's not going to happen now. Ever. As if I ever could.

He looked at Big Mac. "So I guess it's personal after all." And headed back to his truck.

FARMER'S MARKET

"I pulled those out of the ground especially for you this morning," Jill said, sitting on an upturned bucket behind the row of tables. The city woman in her white sundress, matching straw hat, smiled down at her. Picked up a stalk of garlic from the bundle and held it upright like a drum beater. Waved it a couple of times at her companion, a man in a linen suit. They laughed, looked at her to see if she laughed too. Then the woman put it back, gave the slightest shake of her head to her companion, and the two strolled on, along the row of stalls. Visions in white. Figures in the crowd.

The other farms along the way had much larger spreads than Jill's. Some worked out of the back of box trucks, with matching tables, awnings. Plastic bags with the farm's name. Her spread was a mismatch of old card tables, wobbly things, covered with a red-and-white checkerboard plastic cloth. Maybe if she wore an apron. She could embroider a name on it, though their farm didn't really have one. It was always just the Nichols Place.

While she waited, she sorted through the cardboard tags she'd made, putting them in order, *$1, $2, 2 for $3*. Laying them out by color and denomination like a game of solitaire. It had been a bad spring for them. Cold, and hard rains, hail even. She looked at her small piles of produce. The zucchini was pockmarked like nicked wood. Her lettuce was shredded by the last storm, pieces of leaves scattered over their fields like confetti. The peas and green beans weren't bad, though. And her prices were good, but she couldn't go much lower, she wouldn't be able to afford the gas for their van to get here each week.

"Do you have any corn?" A woman in a housedress peered at her.

"Sorry, the corn won't be in for another month."

"Well, I'm sure somebody here has some. If you don't." Clomped away.

Jill stared at the cards in front of her a long time. *$4. 3 for $4.* With her fingertips she traced a curve through her hair to reset it behind her ear. Smoothed Jim's plaid shirt down over her front. Maybe if she started to wear a little lipstick, or tied a pretty ribbon in her hair.

STRAIGHTENING UP

"There's still a lot of ham and potato salad left. The Jell-O salad went in a hurry."

"It usually does."

"We covered everything and put it in the fridge."

Ellie just wanted the woman to leave. She needed to be alone. Wanted to be.

"And you have my number."

"Always have," Ellie said. Then hoped it didn't sound the way it came out.

"That's right," Elizabeth said, gathering up her purse, the Bible she carried to the service. "And don't you hesitate to use it, if you need anything in this hour of travail."

Ellie followed Elizabeth to the door and watched her cross the yard to her car and drive away. Thank heavens. Hour of travail. Where did she get such phrases? Ellie wandered through the downstairs of the house, straightening up after the dozens of people who had appeared for the funeral dinner. People she hadn't seen for years. She supposed she should have been bitter—where were they over the years, when she would have liked to see them?—but she was too glad to see them now. She put the straight chairs back in their places at the table, adjusted the pictures on the mantel, the ones of Fred and of Fred and her that they had taken to display at the funeral home. Then she stood at the front window, looking through the sheers at the front yard. The barn and the sheds across the way.

He had already sold the place, knowing he was sick, so she wouldn't have to worry. So she'd be taken care of. Sad, in a way, she would have liked to try to run it on her own, she always thought she could. Hire the right hands, it wouldn't have been hard. Well, the arrangements had been made, she could go on living here, until it was her time too. That was good of him. He had been a good man. She didn't think she'd miss him all that much, it would be a relief in a way, once she got used to the quiet. But she would have missed this view, the hills, the solitary oak in the field. The breeze along the porch.

ONE FOR SORROW

There was a crow in the hickory wood. Somewhere over the hill. Calling, calling. *One for sorrow, two for mirth; three for a marriage, four for a birth. . . .*

She had sung the rhyme to her baby in the weeks after she brought it home, her little Elizabeth. So tiny, so trusting. Flesh of my flesh. Her baby, her own. She sang now. *Five for laughing, six for crying. . . .*

The social worker at the hospital questioned whether she should try to raise the baby. Barry, the boy who did the thing to her, didn't want any part of it, or of her. But that was okay. She had showed them, showed them all. Her mom and dad didn't say anything when they learned the baby was due. Reacted no differently than if one of the cows had dropped an unexpected calf. Another creature to raise, to take care of. Her parents would be back from the fair today. They would want to know.

Seven for sickness, eight for dying. . . .

Mary Elizabeth sat on the swing on her parents' front porch. The breeze drifting slowly back and forth, back and forth. She looked at the baby cradled in her meaty arm. Flesh the color of her flesh. She giggled and lifted her loose top up around her shoulders, placed the naked child on her belly. Like another roll of her flesh. She lifted one of the legs by the big toe, which wasn't big at all. Lifted the leg and dropped it. Lifted and dropped. The lifeless leg, the miniature foot falling on her tummy as gentle as a love pat. Then thought she shouldn't play with it. Pulled down her top again and cradled the baby again.

Nine for silver, ten for gold, eleven for a secret that will never be told. . . .

She had carried the baby with her for two days now, since the first night after her parents left for the fair. Left her and the baby alone. Since she had taken the baby to bed with her when the baby wouldn't stop crying. A comfort. Since she woke the next morning and found it under her, like another roll of her flesh. She had carried it with her on the chance it might breathe and cry again. Now she sat with her baby on the porch looking out over the sweep of the fields and the hills. Waiting for their pickup to appear at the top of the lane. Listening to the crow in the hickory wood. Wondering, Crow, why can't you sing a song for me?

LOST AND FOUND

"I thought you'd be mowing," Donna said as she passed behind the counter.

"I should be," Dave said. Pushed his John Deere cap further back on his head.

The waitress acknowledged the remark with a slight up-nod and kept going. When she came back she took out her pad and pencil and began to write.

"The sausage here isn't as good as the other place. But the ham's better."

"Then I'll take the ham."

"I knew that." She tapped the pencil once on the pad for emphasis, gave him a smartass smile, and hung his check on the order wheel in the window to the kitchen. The cook looked at the check, looked at Dave, and went back to work. In a few moments she returned with the coffeepot. Looked him in the eyes as she filled his mug.

"So. Why aren't you? Mowing? You've got fields that need it."

"Do you know how many coffee shops and restaurants there are in this area?" Dave said, meeting her eyes.

"It didn't take you too long to go down the list." She cocked her head, raised her eyebrows at him as she finished pouring his cup, then headed back down the counter. He watched her as she moved about the restaurant, the familiar juggle of her ass inside the tight white dress. The easy smile as she bantered with farmers and truck drivers, older couples out for breakfast. Thinking, She knows the farm. She's been by it. Why? When she came back with his food, he said, "It must have been pretty sudden, you leaving the other place."

"No, actually I'd been thinking of it for a while."

"You didn't say anything to me about it."

"Maybe I wanted to see if you'd go to the trouble to find me." And she was gone again. He stared at the plate of food in front of him, wondering if what she said was true. He thought that tracking her down would prove something, but now he wasn't sure what it was, or to whom. Finding her didn't answer what he was going to do about it, about her. What he was going to do about a wife and three kids and fields he could leave that needed mowing.

FURROW AND SLICE

Cam followed the track of his last furrow, followed the contour of the slope of the hill, the tractor pulling easily through the field of wild grass he had left idle for several seasons, giving the field a rest. Somewhere he had a photo of his father plowing this same field with a horse. When he was just a boy, about Robert's age. That day.

Robert had brought his graduation pictures over for Cam and Maddie to see. The boy was so proud. He had just told them about a girl he liked. Brought her picture too.

He made the corner, started down the short side, working toward the center, when he saw the rabbit bolt away in front of him. There must have been a nest but there was no hope for it now. There never was. Against his better judgment he looked back.

Then the boy got a look on his face. Like he just heard something from a long ways off. He stood up. Said, "Grandpa." And collapsed.

The little bodies were scattered up the sides of the furrow as if hit with a bomb. Cam stopped the tractor, put it in neutral, set the brake. Got down and walked slowly back along the slice. A few were bleeding from various wounds. Others twitched, stunned. None had their eyes open. Cam picked up each one and in turn wrenched its neck.

He caught the boy and laid him on the linoleum. Ellie was crying, "Call the doctor, call the ambulance!" If there was breath—was there breath?—it wasn't apparent.

He noticed it out of the corner of his eye. One of the rabbits had made it into the next furrow, struggling in the loose soil as it tried to get away. Cam bent down and picked it up.

He slapped Robert's face, repeatedly, calling his name. Ellie cried, "Cam, we have to get help!" But Cam kept on. Calling him, calling. As if, if he could just get the boy to pay attention, he wouldn't die. But he did anyway.

The mother wouldn't touch it now, with the smell of a human on it. In Cam's pinch of fingers, the tiny rabbit's legs worked furiously, swimming in midair. He brushed the dirt from its blind eyes, cleared away the last grains with a puff of his breath. The rabbit stopped struggling, as if it heard something from a long ways off.

THE EASY PART

"The farm's been in the family for seven generations," Clay said.

"Eight," Bruce said. "You don't have to remind me."

"You've seen the inscription scratched on that beam. 1854."

"Yes, and I don't care to see it again." Bruce nudged a small dent in the dust with the toe of his shoe. Gazed off toward the hills. "Look, this isn't about all that."

"Yes. It is."

Clay looked in the direction Bruce was looking. He wondered what his brother saw, if they saw the same hills. It didn't seem like it. Clay loved every inch of this land. Knew every inch of this land. Had worked every inch.

"Look around, Clay. You've got subdivisions on three sides. Now that Wilson sold his place. You can see the new homes going up from here."

"What do Ben and Tillie say?"

"Would it matter what the rest of the family thinks?"

"Never did," Clay grinned. He was a head shorter than his brother, built like their father, not so much all muscle as sinew. That the one who stayed to work the place was now considered a stumbling block to the family's future was an irony not lost on Clay. But that wasn't it at all.

"Look at this place, Clay. It's falling down around your ears."

"We've had a couple tough years. But I think this one may get us out of the hole."

"We'll fight you, you know that."

"I know that." Clay studied the faded pattern down the front of his flannel shirt.

"And we'll win. God, Clay, I've got an entire law firm that can. . . ."

"And I've got cows that need milked."

Bruce shook his head and, threading his way among the droppings, headed back to his SUV. As his brother drove away, Clay raised his hand but the other didn't acknowledge it. In the barn the cows were lowing, he recognized Lucy, but he took a moment to look at the hills again, the fields. Bruce wouldn't understand. Giving up was the easy part. He smiled to himself and turned back to the barn. Thinking, Hold on, girls. I'm on my way.

BE STILL MY HEART

One

"Don't laugh, it's not funny," Mary Beth said. "If something happened to you, I'd be the one who had to come in and clean out all this mess."

Mary Elizabeth pooh-poohed her. "You don't have to concern yourself. I'm not going anywhere," she said, a cigarette dangling from the edge of her mouth as she moved one pile of papers on top of another. Speaking through a haze of her own smoke. "They'd have to drag me out of here."

But sure enough, that's what they did, all right. Dragged her out of here, or at least carried her, the only resistance being the force of gravity on deadweight. When Mary Beth hadn't heard from her for several days, she came over and let herself in with the extra key Mary Elizabeth kept under the John Deere rain gauge in the yard. Found Mary Elizabeth lying spread-eagle in the middle of the living room floor among some stacks of old newspapers and *Ladies' Home Journals*. Heart attack. Mary Elizabeth's fingers bloodied to the bone and a good-sized chunk missing from her cheek from where the half dozen cats she kept in the house started to nibble on her. Just barn cats really, wild things that Mary Elizabeth took in whenever one showed up at the door. Poor things, Mary Beth thought, they just got hungry. She didn't blame them, didn't blame them in the least.

Now here she was, just as she said she'd be, was afraid she'd be, left to clean out the place, the double-wide trailer. She looked around, wondering where to start. From the other end of the double-wide came the creak of a floorboard. "Hello?" she said. Her voice sounding small. Muffled as if smothered under a blanket. "Is somebody there?"

Two

"I might be able to use these for something," Mary Elizabeth said, wadding up the remnants from where they were cutting out dress patterns in home ec class and sticking them in her schoolbag. Mary Beth could hear Mary Elizabeth say it as if it happened yesterday, she heard her say it so often through the years. It wouldn't surprise her if she found those very remnants somewhere in the house in a box marked *Cloth Not Worth Saving.*

Mary Elizabeth and Mary Beth. Two Mary Elizabeths actually, though the latter accepted the diminutive to help tell them apart. Because they were alike in other ways too, though more in the nature of complementaries rather than identicals. Mary Elizabeth as blond and fair as Mary Beth was dark and coarse-featured. Mary Elizabeth as pleasingly plump as Mary Beth was rail thin. Mary Elizabeth as bold as Mary Beth was acquiescent.

They were on a Sunday school field trip, sitting together on the bus as they always did, when they noticed Dan Thomas sitting up front with Jennifer Collins. "You just wait," Mary Elizabeth said. "He'll be sitting with me on the way home. And then it'll be dark."

Sure enough, on the way home Mary Elizabeth sat with Dan, leaving Mary Beth to sit with Jennifer. Who sat facing the window so no one would see she was crying.

"How did you get him to sit with you?" Mary Beth said when she caught up with her friend back at the church. Mary Elizabeth swung along, in and out of the shadows of the tree-lined walk. "I told him he could put his hand up under my sweater."

They giggled and scrunched together as they walked along. Twins girls of different mothers. Though it occurred to Mary Beth now that among all the clutter Mary Elizabeth left of her life she might find Dan's remains in a box marked *Men No Longer Useful.*

Three

Mary Beth wondered if Mary Elizabeth's pack-rat tendencies might change after she was married. Ben was twenty years her senior, a man who had been married once before and swore he'd never marry again, which held until Mary Elizabeth sashayed along. As Mary Elizabeth explained to Mary Beth, Ben was the perfect prospect for her—an older man to support her in a way to which she would like to become accustomed. And the man had a house. No matter that the man wasn't much to look at. No matter that the house wasn't much to look at either—a 150-year-old farmhouse. It would still be a place of her own, a place that she could do with as she liked. Perhaps Mary Beth should have guessed what was going on in Mary Elizabeth's mind by the way she always said his name as if spelled "Bin."

When Mary Elizabeth moved in, the house was a shambles. Ben's first wife didn't so much accumulate things, it was more that she never threw anything away. That, and she never cleaned. A layer of dust an eighth of an inch thick covered everything. As Ben told Mary Beth, "I 'spect Mary Elizabeth can put this place to rights soon enough." To her credit, Mary Elizabeth—with Mary Beth's help, of course—went through the house and cleaned it top to bottom. But rather than throw out all the stuff accumulated from Ben's first marriage, she proceeded to add to it. Her stuffed animals, stacks of fan magazines, seemingly every article of clothing she'd ever worn, boxes of unnamed stuff, such as the remnants from her home ec classes. And new things she bought and picked up here and there, the clutter appearing to multiply exponentially. Ben looked on in wonder, and eventually dismay. As he later told Mary Beth, "I knew I was in trouble when she brought home two old toilet bowls to use as flowerpots on the front steps. It was all downhill from there."

She could swear she heard someone moving at the other end of the house.

Four

Maybe a squirrel or field mouse, even a raccoon, had gotten into the house, maybe that's what she kept hearing. Mary Beth wandered through this end of the double-wide like a visitor at an exhibition. Dining room, kitchen, living room. Down the short hallway off the kitchen to the bathroom and back. The smell of cat urine overwhelming, all-pervasive, the cat pans overflowing with feces like sand-speckled Tootsie Rolls. From the road at the top of the lane came the occasional hum of a car going past. She didn't turn on any lights, the sunlight through the windows providing light enough. What she couldn't see, she didn't need to, at least for now.

In the gloom, genealogy charts were spread out over the dining room table. Mary Elizabeth's never-ending search for the roots of it all, where her family came from, maybe clues as to where it was headed. In the sunporch Mary Elizabeth called her study were piles of old Sunday school lessons, inspirational books, collections of hymns. She picked up a book called *The Gospel of the Hammer*, put it back on top of *A Child's Collection of Psalms*. What did it all come to? Fodder for refuge boxes. Stuff for rummage and yard sales.

She thought of her own house. Her own meager collection of things. Her house as neat and clean as Mary Elizabeth's was cluttered and chaotic. Who would clean out her things after she was gone? Who would note her on a genealogy chart? A dead branch.

She had been the dutiful daughter. Devoting herself to tending the long death of first her grandparents when her own parents were no longer strong enough to help them. Then in turn her father, her mother. In turn, cleaning out her grandparents', then her own parents' houses. A witness as it were at the closing of other people's lives. She noticed her reflection standing among the figures of another family's portrait. She took a step and it was gone.

Five

Mary Elizabeth never asked Mary Beth to help around the house. It was more or less assumed that she would, expected perhaps, their relationship being what it was. It started naturally enough when Mary Elizabeth came home from the hospital with their first- (and only) born, a boy they named Billy. It was a rough delivery and Mary Elizabeth was bed-ridden for weeks afterward. Mary Beth, when she came over to visit mother and child, would fix meals, and then somebody was needed to wash all those diapers, and mix and heat up all the bottles of formula, and Ben needed clean clothes, and somebody needed to feed the chickens and gather the eggs, and there were errands that needed to be run, and the more she looked at the dust and clutter around the place the less Mary Beth could stand it, it was no place for a baby. Before she knew it she was part of the household, an expected presence—"Oh, Mary Beth can do that when she comes by"—spending her days traveling back and forth between Mary Elizabeth's and her own grandmother at one location and her other grandmother at another and her mother and father and occasionally even stopping by her own place to do something for herself.

And then the baby died. Suddenly. At seven months, alive just long enough to develop a Billy-personality. Mary Elizabeth put the baby in his crib after his middle-of-the-night feeding. In the morning, she found him there snuffed out. Beyond recovery, either for the baby or for Mary Elizabeth. She returned to her bed and that was where Mary Beth found them when she arrived that morning, each in their own bed, Billy dead for hours and something inside of Mary Elizabeth rapidly dying. And there in her bed was where Mary Elizabeth stayed most of the time for years to come. As if the velocity of life's whirl pinned her there.

Six

And there was Ben. Hard working, salt-of-the-earth, do-any-thing-for-you, totally clueless Ben. Mary Elizabeth didn't so much marry him as add him to her stuff. Mary Beth never cared for her friend's husband that much—oh, he was nice enough, and nice enough to her. It was his looks. His lips were nearly non-existent, as if sucked inside his mouth by the force of an inner vacuum. It made him appear smug, which was unfortunate be-cause it was quite apparent from everything else about him—especially as soon as he opened his mouth—that he had nothing to be smug about. But as it turned out, most of Mary Beth's involvement with him didn't require her to look at him.

She was down on her hands and knees one day scrubbing the kitchen—Mary Elizabeth was upstairs in her bed as usual—when Ben came in from the fields for lunch. "Looks like the south end of Mary Beth headed north," he said, washing his hands at the sink behind her. She looked over her shoulder at him and wiggled her ass. Meaning only to be playful. But in the moment's pause that followed they both knew what was going to happen.

He knelt behind her, worked her sweatpants down to expose her ass, freed one leg and then mounted her, coming into her surprisingly gentle she thought, she had braced herself for the worst, for him to slam into her, rutting like barnyard animals, the stud bulls she had seen, humping her with terrible rhythmic insistent violence, but instead he was slow but nonetheless intense, intent, as if he was savoring her, making it last as long as possible for himself, the act and the experience itself, the gasp he gave when he finally came equaled by the spasms that wracked through her, taking her own breath away.

Seven

They came together—there was no other term for it, it certainly wasn't love; maybe desire had something to do with it, but it didn't include attraction—several times a week in the beginning, for maybe four or five years, then less later on, once a week, then once a month or so, finally just occasionally, a few times a year, but always in the same way, like animals still (she didn't want to look at him for one thing, didn't want to see his face, and she definitely didn't want to kiss him), he would come up behind her or if they met face-on he would put his hand on her pelvis and gently turn her around, bend her over the sink or a table, the back of a chair or if they were in the barn over a stable rail, work her pants and panties off and begin the slow steady revolving rhythm that seemed to be their own, almost like a kind of dance that despite its anonymity carried with it a certain tenderness and caring, not necessarily for the being of the other person but for the act of being itself, a recognition of shared or similar trials and worries and disappointments, the stuff of being alive, sentient creatures, the release when it finally came a celebration of being alive, each in their own and separate worlds, a triumph of the spirit if you will, of making the best with what was offered to them, then breaking away and going on with whatever it was they were doing in the first place, their meetings never planned but always accepted when they happened.

It went on this way for years, Mary Elizabeth still upstairs in her bed or at least somewhere else in the house when her husband

and her best friend shared whatever it was they shared. Then, because he was older to begin with, Ben grew old and fell ill and was dying, all before Mary Beth quite knew it was happening. She went to him once in his final days, the man barely alive in the hospital bed they installed in the living room, but he opened his eyes and smiled and managed to whisper, "I almost didn't recognize you from this end."

Eight

And just like that, after Ben was diagnosed with inoperable cancer—it wasn't only one, it turned out to be several; he was being eaten alive from the inside out—and died within a few weeks' time, Mary Elizabeth, who had spent the last two decades in bed or at least dressed in bedclothes to signify to her husband or Mary Beth or anyone else who happened to be around, such as the hairdresser who came in once a month and even the doctor who made house calls, that she might be out of bed at the moment but she was headed back there again soon, got up and resumed her life as if nothing had happened.

In a few months, Mary Elizabeth sold the farm and bought the new double-wide that she had placed on a slope overlooking the old place. Mary Beth wondered what Mary Elizabeth would ever do with all the space in her new home—there were four bathrooms and three bedrooms, two living areas and a formal dining room—but she should have known. Mary Elizabeth's collecting tendencies had been more or less on hold during her bedridden years, so much so that Mary Beth almost forgot about them, thinking that perhaps Mary Elizabeth had forgotten about them too. Silly goose. Fortified by the money Ben left in his will and the sale of the property, Mary Elizabeth seemed to be on a mission to fill up her new home as quickly as she could, bringing with her everything from the old house and adding to it everything she could think of. Things seemed to multiply in the new place, boiling out of cardboard boxes—she kept those too—

spreading throughout the rooms. She even bought Ben's hospital bed they rented for his last days at home and installed it in one of the bedrooms, piling it high with boxes of his clothes. The IV stand became a clothes rack; the oxygen tanks were used to display the caps he used to wear.

Now she was certain she heard someone moving at the other end of the house.

Nine

"Get me a cup of coffee, would you?" Mary Elizabeth said, studying the wall of dominos facing her, the few tiles left in the boneyard between them.

Mary Beth looked at her from behind her own wall of tiles. Finally she said, "You know, waiting on you while you were bed-ridden was one thing. But now that you're up and about, it's another matter."

The two women sat across from each other at the table in the breakfast nook. Mary Elizabeth with her back to the wall of windows. Though she could still see the farm and her old house on the opposite hill if she turned her head.

"You're closer," Mary Elizabeth said. "Besides, that's what you do, isn't it?"

"What do I do? Get people coffee?"

"Service people. You sure you don't have any eights?" Mary Elizabeth said. Then looked at her. "That's when you're happiest, servicing people. Like Ben."

"What about Ben?" Mary Beth said softly, looking at her hands. Did Mary Elizabeth know about her and Ben? She supposed Mary Elizabeth was right, that is what Mary Beth did all those years, service his desires. She had thought that it had something to do with her. That it was hers, what she and Ben did together. But maybe it was his, she was just the device, the attendant, the occasion. Maybe all along it had been Mary Elizabeth's, knowing about it, letting it go on because then she didn't have to do it. "What about Ben?"

"I mean, like Ben used to be with animals. He was happiest when he was taking care of his cows. What did you think I meant?"

"No, I don't have any eights," Mary Beth said quietly. Got up to get the coffee.

"Then I guess it's a draw, isn't it?" Mary Elizabeth said and smiled.

Ten

She saw it out of the corner of her eye, at least she thought she saw it, saw something, a glint or shadow passing quickly down the hallway, slipping into a doorway at the far end. Maybe it was a reflection from a car passing along the road. But how, with no windows nearby? A ghost or spirit? Mary Elizabeth come back to haunt her? Hadn't she haunted Mary Beth enough while she was alive? The thought surprised her, it never occurred to her before that the relationship she had with the person she called her best friend might be considered in such a way. Or maybe it was Ben, come back to find his rented hospital death bed. He had haunted her too in life, though in a different way. Such thoughts did little to ease her mind.

There was movement in one of the bedrooms, she was sure of it. Mary Elizabeth's room. The shadow of a tree outside the window, moving in the wind? She wasn't sure. You heard of such things, a single woman alone in a house, surprising an intruder and paying the price. A victim of circumstance. Or maybe she was just another pathetic older woman, victim of her own circumstances. Haunted by her fantasies.

"I had desires too," she said out loud, shouted down the hallway. "I wanted things too. I'm more than just another fancy plate hanging on the wall. More than just a figurine on a shelf. More than something to put in a stack with all the other stuff you've used up but keep around just so nobody else can have it."

There was no response. Nothing moved. And she knew there was nothing there. No one. There never had been. Never would be. She turned and fled the house, hurried out the door, not bothering to lock it behind her. Afraid for her life.

How Now Black Cow

"Thanks for coming, Doc. I tried McGallagher, he's my regular vet, but. . . ."

"That her up the hill?" the young man said. He looked at the snow-laden sky but decided against his coat. He took his bag from his Land Cruiser and headed up the slope.

"I called as soon as I looked out this morning and saw her," Logan lurched after him. Simian-like, not so much walking as throwing his weight forward with each step. "I tried to get her in the pen last night, but she dodged away at the last minute. Couldn't get her cornered again. I figured whatever was going to happen was going to happen."

The young man was already on hands and knees at the rear of the fallen cow by the time Logan got there. The vet rolled up his sleeves, doused his hands with alcohol. Began digging with one hand deep inside her. "There's no time. . . ."

"Last year a cow stepped on me. You'd think I'd know better but I got underneath her and it happened. Crushed my femur. I've got pins and screws from my knee to my hip. The same thing they did with Barbaro. Only I sure ain't no thoroughbred. . . ."

The vet had worked one of the calves around so its head was half-out. Logan knelt and helped him pull. The calf popped free with a great sucking sound. A little bull.

"Get the liquid out of its mouth and nostrils. I'll try to get the other one turned."

"I was sure there had to be twins," Logan said. "We're about twelve hours too late, if a calf don't drop when she's ready they get mucus in their lungs. I was afraid she'd breech but I just couldn't get her in the pen. Can't move like I used to. I even came out later hoping she'd find her way back but I lost her in the dark. Then this morning she was down—"

"Will you stop talking so I can think! Stop talking!" The young man had the calf halfway out but it was stillborn and wouldn't budge. The cow raised its head wide-eyed and fell back, its last breath a moan. The little bull was gasping, drowning from within. The young vet sat in the grass amid the three black bodies, helpless, frantic. "Just stop talking!"

Logan didn't respond. He had learned a long time ago to let people say whatever it was they had a mind to, just let them go. The vet was too young to know that in this world of suffering and death there were only words. On a good day. Logan turned and lurched heavily back down the slope, to get the tractor and drag the carcasses away.

PIGLETS AT PLAY

Their squeals filled the barn. Michael leaned on the top rail of the pen, watching four of the surviving piglets take turns sliding on their bellies down the length of a smooth plank lying in the straw; the fifth sat in the corner, watching the others. Someone came through the open door at the far end, a silhouette befitting a large man though he recognized Sis.

"You put the board in there for them?" Sis said, joining him at the rail.

Michael nodded. "You talking about Lori made me think of it."

"You and Lori used to set up a slide like that for them when you were kids."

"Remember the time that farrow just didn't get it? Lori had to go in and throw the first couple of piglets down the board to get them started."

"I remember the mother pig didn't like Lori throwing her piglets around and went after her. And you had to go in and rescue her."

"Old Betsy. I never liked that pig, and that pig never liked me. I have to say it was a real pleasure when it came time for my dad to truss her up and slit her throat."

"She was one nasty pig," Sis said. "But she was sure good eating."

The two of them—the man in his thirties, the older spinster; both dressed in identical denim; both with soup-bowl haircuts, one starting to gray, the other already there—watched the piglets at play in silence. The fifth piglet left its corner and came over and sat in front of them, sitting sidesaddle on its haunches, looking up at them.

"Lori's up at the house now. Her and her husband."

"She seem happy?"

Sis nodded. "She met him at the bank where she works. Seems nice enough."

Michael nodded. Looked at the piglet looking up at him. Its hind legs folded daintily beneath it. Trying not to think about the color of its flesh.

"I'm going back up there now," Sis said, letting go of the railing. "If you wanted to come along and say hello."

Michael smiled, shook his head. Turned away to get back to work. He wanted to ask Sis to tell Lori that he wished her well, but he didn't have the words.

AMERICAN DREAM

"So, where were you? I could have used you."

Don didn't say anything, and Dan didn't expect him to. At least the boy didn't lie. Dan reminded himself his son was no boy, though he wasn't a man in his book either. Despite his age, late twenties. By Dan's standards, a man was a stand-up person, someone who did the right thing. He loved the boy but knew he couldn't count on him. He checked the power take-off to the baler once again, then climbed over the hitch and up onto the tractor.

"They're calling us back," Don said looking out across the field.

"Who's they? Who's us? Where's back?" But Dan thought he knew.

"The Guard. They're sending us back to Iraq. Or maybe Afghanistan."

It was Dan's turn not to say anything. He saw the *Evening News*, he was afraid of this. "When do you report?"

"End of the month."

Dan nodded and took his seat behind the wheel. So the boy took the opportunity to get drunk or stoned or whatever he was up to these days. Another excuse. But what would you expect from someone with an abuse problem who takes an apartment over a bar? Who joined the Guard because he thought it would be easy money, that he'd never have to serve.

"Did you tell your mother?"

"Not yet."

Dan started the tractor. Thought a moment. Then looked down at him. "You missed the mowing. You want to help bale?"

Don grinned and jumped up on the tractor. Dan had always imagined his boys working the farm with him. Then the eldest was killed in a car accident, the boy's own fault. And he was glad his youngest was going back in the Army, the boy needed that structure even though it might get him killed. But as they headed on the tractor out of the yard, his son standing beside him, he could almost pretend he was living his dream.

BEYOND THE DOOR

As he left the house and headed down the slope, the two border collies, Daisy and Duke, fell in beside him, happy to be on a mission, suspecting it had something to do with the calves. Clair disliked keeping the animals in the small barn—it was more of an old shed—but that was the way of it, there was no other place to keep them until they were old enough to join the heifers in the upper field. Through the broken slats the whiteface watched them approach. He could hear them stirring on the other side of the door.

"Stay," he told the dogs, and slipped inside. The dogs looked at each other as if to say, *We know that.*

The structure was dark, windowless, the only light coming from the cracks in the walls, the broken slats he never had time to patch. The barn's dirt floor was more of a sludge hole, a thick mixture of manure and urine and straw and mud from the runoff up the hill that didn't drain properly. The air dank, fetid. The cows stood in a row at the far end of the barn, watching him, watching for the dogs. Ghostly figures in the gloom, the sludge from the floor matted into their hides.

"It's a big day for you girls," Clair said as he waded through the sludge and slid open the door to the upper field. "Time to join the herd."

Sunlight crowded through the opening. A glimpse of the open fields and the further hills. The cows shifted uneasily but stayed where they were. "Move! Go! Get going!" Clair yelled, clapped his hands. When the cows continued to stay put, he waded back to the man door and let the dogs in. Daisy and Duke bounded through the sludge, barking and nipping at the calves' heels. The cows stared wide-eyed at the open door, shifting, lifting their legs away from the dogs. But wouldn't move. Stayed where they were. Lowing. Moaning with fear. And for the briefest instant Clair could almost understand why. An intimation of something at the far edge of his awareness. But whatever it was flitted away just as quickly, and he reached for the prod.

BY ALL RIGHTS

"City water tastes funny."

The young woman with a clipboard smiled as if she knew better.

"It's got chemicals in it," Curt said, sitting on the glider on his front porch.

The young woman—she was just a girl, mid-twenties he guessed—put one foot up on the front steps, trying for casual. "That's to make it safe."

"My water's safe enough for me. Always has been."

"That doesn't mean it always will be. Safe."

"It doesn't mean it won't be, either. Safe."

She smiled and looked away, watched the crows flying off from the fields. "Wells are drying up, going bad all over the region. This project will make sure you always have water."

"This water belongs to this land. We don't need water from someplace else."

"What about sewage?"

"Got all the sewage I can handle. Don't need you bringing in any more."

She laughed in spite of herself. She was cute as a button in her jeans and boots and green safety vest, blond hair curling out from under her county hard hat. But no matter.

"I've got a sand pile that works just fine, thank you very much."

"A sand pile down there by the creek. It's just a matter of time before it leaches into the water table. If it doesn't contaminate your water supply, it will your neighbors'."

"And if your pipe breaks, I've got a lot of other people's sewage to deal with."

"The county needs these water and sewage lines to bring in development."

"That's a good enough argument in my book for keeping them out."

"We'll be back, you know," she said.

"I expect you'll try. And if you set foot on my land again I'll shoot you."

She laughed. Curt laughed too. Then raised an imaginary rifle and sighted down the barrel at her, took careful aim right between her pretty blue eyes. And into those eyes there crept an awareness that he meant it.

Heigh-Ho Come to the Fair

"Does your family sleep in here and everything?" the boy named Justin said. Looking in at the old sofa and kitchen table and chairs her family brought each year to outfit the stall, the floor lamps and the knickknacks her mother kept in a box to make it seem more homey.

"We have a fifth-wheel up on the hill," Britney said. Pleased the city boy didn't know what she meant. "But somebody sleeps down here every night, to keep an eye on them."

He looked down the aisle at the row of boney haunches, the cows lying in the straw in the afternoon heat. Then he glanced back to the other end of the barn, at his half a dozen friends sitting on a feed box. City boys all dressed in black, trying to do Goth she supposed, though none went beyond black eyeliner. The boy called Justin with a black Megadeth T-shirt. Though she did like the spiked dog collar on his wrist. Liked it for her dog.

"Come on, I'll show you something else."

He glanced again at his buddies. Britney saw their giggles, the sucking gestures. She led the way out the side door and across to another show barn. The interior was darker with the horse stalls; when he hesitated while his eyes adjusted, she took his hand. She could imagine what he was thinking. She guided him over to one of the stalls, where a palomino gnawed at a well-gnawed groove in the top of the gate.

"This is Romeo," she told Justin. "Go ahead, pet him. He knows me."

Justin was afraid of looking afraid but she knew he was. Romeo knew it too. As soon as the boy reached for his nose the horse nickered and Justin juked away. Britney grinned.

"I'm going back. Uh, thanks." Justin stumbled back across the rutted floor and out into daylight. She could imagine his friends. "Did she? Did she do it?" She saw the city kids each year, the groups with their latest iPods and cell phones, texting as they sauntered past. Thinking they were so cool. So much better than she was. She rubbed Romeo's nose again, and walked on through the barn to where her family sat outside around a picnic table, her mom watching her soaps on the portable TV, her dad with his braces off his shoulders drinking a beer, her brother and sisters playing Yahtzee.

"We was just saying," her dad said, leaning on one arm of his aluminum chair. "Brit wishes it was fair time all the time, don't you, Brit?"

She ducked her head and smiled and knew he was right. And wondered why she felt something deep inside her sink.

THE VERY IDEA

She landed hard on the hard floor and for a moment—was it only a moment?—lost track of where she was. Slowly she became aware that she was lying on a cold concrete floor, in the dark, and that her hip hurt. Badly. What if it were broken? What was that statistic about elderly people with broken hips dying within the year? What did a broken hip feel like? She only knew her hip hurt like heck.

It gradually came to her that she was at the church. The church basement as a matter of fact. How did she get here? Oh yes, that came to her too. They were having a meeting of the liturgy committee. And things were going along nicely, as they always did, discussing the sermons and the lessons for the next month or so. And then out of nowhere that Marge Garvin said, "I think we need to address this issue of the flowers."

"What issue with what flowers?" Millie said.

"Well, a group of us have been talking. And we don't think it's proper to have the flowers on the altar. We think they should be down in front of the altar."

Well, who ever heard of such a thing? Millie had taken care of the flowers for years, picking them from her garden or in winter picking them out at the florist, arranging them in their twin brass vases and placing them just so on either side of the cross between the candles. She knew what this was about. It was the new people. People from the city moving out here to the country. Who didn't know the history, the way things had always been, who wanted to change things just to change things. Millie was so upset she couldn't talk to anyone after the meeting, didn't want to even be with them. Took the narrow back steps, she must have tripped on the way down and here she was.

She could hear them still talking upstairs. But she wasn't going to give them the satisfaction. Her hip hurting more than ever, unable to stand, she started to pull herself by her elbows across the floor, the sleeves of her summer blouse providing no cushion against the stone-hard concrete, the skin on her elbows rubbed raw, the bones of her forearms aching within a few yards, got to the basement door and stretched up, managed somehow to push the panic bar and got herself outside, the sounds of the choir practicing "A Mighty Fortress" coming through the open windows, a nighthawk whistling across the evening sky, inched her way down the concrete steps and across the gravel drive, her blouse torn now and bloody, crying now, her hip alive with pain, thinking, If Bill was here he'd know what to do, why did he have to die, why did he have to die without me, thinking, Help me, O Lord, thy handmaiden.

HOME IS WHERE

He could see the house from the top of the hill. Snug among the cluster of oak trees, the barn and the outbuildings tucked in around it. The darkness of the approaching evening already filled the little valley where they lived. That they called home.

He sat on the tractor, the vibrations of the idling engine carrying up to his hands gripping the wheel. She would be in the kitchen now fixing dinner. The television on with the local news. Her hunger as she got older to hear about the latest shooting in Pittsburgh, the latest driver splattered on a late-night highway. The boy would be there too, home from school, sitting at the counter under her watchful eye. The link they shared, of which he seemed to have no part.

He put the tractor in gear, anticipated the jolt as the hay wagon took up the slack of the hitch. Slowly made his way down the trail he cut for himself earlier. He remembered the earlier years, when he could hardly wait to get home, to see her in the evenings. He never entered or left the house without a kiss. Never missed an opportunity to touch her, put his hand on her shoulder or her back or her ass while he watched her working in the kitchen. As he approached the hay barn the cattle came to the fence to watch him pass; the blueticks hallooed from their row of crates, the collie-mix leapt against her chain, knocking herself off balance with her tail-wagging; Maggie the goat stood up to peer at him over the top of her pen. He backed the wagon into position close to the hay feeder where he would drop the bale in the morning. Then turned off the engine, left the tractor where it was.

The quiet enfolded him. He walked a few steps to get the kinks out. Watched the swallows against the lighter sky flit in and away from the barn. In the evening, the house was its own shadow. Light from the windows in the dining room and kitchen spilled out over the ivy, the rhododendrons. He looked at the house a long time. He could feed and water the dogs, that would be something. And there was Maggie. In the dusk her face bobbed ghost-like above the top plank of her pen. As he went to pet her, the animal lifted the crown of her head into the overturned cup of his hand.

FAMILY REUNION

"I always forget how pleasant it is here," Carla said, looking up at the trees.

"Maybe you should come back more often," Cady said.

"Last week at this time I was on the sands of Cozumel," Catherine said.

"Not everyone has a husband who can take them to Cozumel," Carol said.

The sisters sat under the twin oak trees in the side yard, watching their collection of children helping their grandmother redd the picnic benches beside the house. Watching their father hack at weeds along the edge of the fields with an old-fashioned scythe.

"You know, they can't run this place much longer. Dad's already. . . ." Carla said.

"I'm glad you all saw for yourselves last night how he can go off," Cady said. "You talk sometimes like you think I'm exaggerating how he gets these days."

"There's no exaggerating that he threw his plate at the waitress," Carla said.

"I thought I'd die," Catherine said. "My kids don't want to be around him."

"Your kids don't want to be around us," Carol said, motioning to the old farmhouse.

"I'm sorry, but cow manure is a little out of their comfort zone," Catherine said.

"Maybe if they knew something of the world besides private schools," Carol said.

"This isn't going to solve what to do about Dad. He'll only get worse," Cady said.

"Cady's right," Carla said. "We've got to be thinking about where we're going to put him, a home or what. And how we're going to pay for it."

"If that's what this is about, forget it," Catherine said. "Those private schools you're giving me grief about cost plenty, I'll tell you."

"Well, don't look at me," Carol said. "I can't even afford to go to Cozumel."

Cady didn't say anything. She was watching her life play out in front of her. Their father slipping into dementia, their mother working herself into her grave. And because Cady had to live here as a single parent, her own life sinking further and further from her grasp.

"I guess we should be going," Carol said. "We have a long drive back to the city."

"And we have a plane to catch," Catherine said.

MAKING HAY

"I'll be ready in a few minutes," Ellie called from upstairs.

Carl looked at himself one last time in the hall mirror. Wondering if others would see what he did. A weathered—you could say beat-up—older man in a seldom-worn suit. He walked on through the house and out to the front porch.

In the front yard, Buddy, the hound mix, chased a barn swallow back and forth across the grass. Obviously playing with each other, Buddy never leaping ahead to get the bird in one bite, the bird staying low but not too far ahead so the dog wouldn't lose interest. Ellie was surprised when Carl said he'd go to the fiftieth class reunion; in the past he had always chucked the announcements as soon they arrived. Maybe he was surprised too. But fifty years, that was different. That seemed worth something. He left the porch and crossed the yard to the tractor with mower in tow parked under the oak tree. Buddy and the bird played on.

What would they look like now, those kids he knew in high school? Truth was, he knew very few. There were the town kids and the farm kids, the bus kids. Oil and water. He knew the town kids by name only, the school in-group. The only group he belonged to was the Future Farmers of America. The same men he talked to now at the feed store or granary. No one else at the reunion would know him from Adam. He climbed up and sat on the tractor.

What was her name? Kathy something. The prettiest girl in school. Prom queen. The prettiest eyes. Sat behind him in homeroom. She would smile as she passed up the aisle, not really at him but in general, the pleasure of being herself he supposed. He never would presume to speak. Then that day she tapped him on the shoulder. He turned around, the only time. A question about something. And he saw in her eyes: It wasn't that she had ever snubbed him; how could she, he simply wasn't there. He didn't exist in her known world.

He started the tractor and headed across the grass. At the sound of the engine, Buddy came running, ecstatic that they were heading out. Ellie was on the porch as he passed, in her party dress, a look on her face that said she should have guessed. Understood that he would be mowing now, suit go to hell, till long past dark.

KYLE IN WINTER

One

Caleb and Jessie nearly knocked him over in their rush to get out the door and down the side steps into the snow. As Kyle headed up the hill to the lower barn, the two bluetick hounds chased each other in the drifts, burrowed their noses in the snow and tossed it in the air, snapping at the cold. Kyle grinned, but not much. The knot in his lower side was hurting more, not good. In the barn the pain shot through his system when he loaded the bucket of duck chow (it was actually cat food but the ducks didn't know) into the bed of the Mule, a bale of hay for the horses. I know you're there, he said to it. I haven't forgotten you. As he started the Mule and headed down the slope across the yard, Caleb and Jessie trailed behind, each claiming a track in the snow for their own.

The ducks were hurrying out from beneath the front porch, slipping and sliding in the snow to beat him to the pond. The last one slid into the frigid water as he pulled close by, hoisted the five-gallon bucket from the bed of the Mule. As he tossed handfuls of the feed across the pond, poured the rest into a wash-tub on the bank, Caleb and Jessie kept a respectful distance, having learned their lesson from the ducks in the past. He watched the ducks quibble among themselves for the food. Silly birds. He usually turned off the pump for the waterfall when it got this cold, but this time he decided to let it run. Ellie had loved the pond, the waterfall. The ducks. When they brought her home from the hospital for what they knew would be the last time, he mounted the hospital bed on blocks next to the living room window so she could see them as she lay there. Maybe the last thing she ever saw. The knot in his side kicked him. Yes, he told it. I'm glad you waited.

Two

He put the empty bucket back in the bed of the Mule, climbed in behind the wheel. The drive up to the main road still looked passable from when he plowed it this morning. Sarah shouldn't have trouble with her four-wheel drive. On the opposite hill, smoke curled from the triple-wide of the two sisters. He had brought their groceries in yesterday before the storm hit, they should be okay for a couple of days. He started the Mule and bucked his way through the drifts to the drive and headed toward the east pasture. Caleb and Jessie parading behind.

The horses were Julie's idea. Part of the things she did to make the place more her own. Though she hadn't seen fit to take them with her when she took off for Florida. What did she expect? Which meant, what more could he have done to make her stay? He bumped over the drainage ditch, snow flying up and spraying his face, and headed into the field.

She was the pretty girl in the insurance office, the one who was always cheerful and flirty when he'd go in to make payments or change his coverage if he bought or sold his cattle or got new equipment. When Ellie was in the hospital, Julie was helpful in making sure he understood his coverage; when Ellie died, the younger woman helped him get all his payments. She had always been curious about his place, asked him questions about it. It seemed only natural, after an appropriate time had passed, to invite her out to see it for herself. Within a year she started to make trips out every weekend. Then overnights. The way Sarah did now. After they were married, Julie redecorated the entire house. Checkered curtains and machine-made quilts and rustic pine furniture. Like a picture from a country living magazine. When that didn't do it for her, he bought her the palomino. Then the jumper. None of it turned out to be enough. Of whatever it was she wanted.

Three

"But why?" he asked her that night when she told him.

"I just have to go. I just have to get away."

"Are you coming back?"

She sighed and looked at her hands. Her always perfectly manicured hands. "I'm moving there, Kyle. I've got a job there already. And I'm getting my Realtor's license."

"I know you wanted to add on another room. We could do that. . . ."

"It just wasn't the way I thought it was going to be. I don't know. It's so hard here. I thought it would be, I don't know, more colorful. Or something."

"Are you going with somebody else? Is there somebody else?"

She got up and stood beside him. Traced the outline of his ear with the edge of her acrylic nail. Like a small dull knife. "Oh Kyle, you always had the most beautiful hair."

In a way it would have been easier if there had been somebody else. At least that he could understand. Or if she took his money, but she didn't even want half. She just wanted out. To have a different life. As he followed the fence, the Mule fought for traction in the blown snow. The palomino stuck its head out the door of the horse shed to watch him come. Above the stubble of the cornfield the afternoon sun was a blank disk.

He wrestled the bale of hay off the bed of the Mule and inside the horse shed. Dragged it to the middle of the floor, cut the twine, took the pitchfork and broke the bale apart, into rough slices. The horses stood in the doorway from the run, watching him work as if comparing notes. Snuffled steam. Caleb and Jessie, always glad to see their horse friends, stood on their hind legs to peer over the top of the half door. Two speckled-nose heads against the view of the winter fields.

Four

Julie had been the love of his life. If by "love" you meant romance. (He wasn't so sure now that it was.) The first time he experienced the soul-wrenching, gut-clenching emotion he'd always heard about in movies and popular songs. Ellie, on the other hand, was . . . well, Ellie. He had known her all his life, grew up on adjacent farms. Waited together at the top of the lane for the bus through twelve years of school. It was only natural when the time came to pair off that they'd marry. She was like family, unavoidable in a way, and the family grew with them together, a boy and a girl, both gone now to opposite shores of the country. Gone from him in their leaving, each in their own way, as Ellie was gone from him in death. The living turned to memories. Then love, or at least desire—someone interested in him, finally, for whatever reason—came with Julie. His days full of feelings he'd never had before. The younger woman all softness and sweet smells, full of the promise of life. Maybe more had left with her than he first realized.

The palomino, Murphy, gave him a nudge. Breaking his reverie. You're right, Murph, got to keep my mind on what I'm doing. He took the carrots from the pocket of his barn coat. Held one upright as the horse nibbled it down to his fingertips, then a second. He rubbed its pale muzzle, up the stiff hair on its face and forehead. I know you miss her. He wished he could say the same. But once she said she didn't want to be here, he didn't want her here. Considered her gone, as dead to him as Ellie. Tux, the jumper, was holding back, as he always did, but stood quivering as Kyle approached, quickly snatched the offered carrot and turned away. Smart horse, he thought, not to trust. Just because I feed you every day.

Five

Miserable bastard! The knot clenched as he climbed off the tractor to close the gate behind him to the cattle pen. You won't let
me forget for a minute, will you? Caleb and Jessie took seats up
the slope, having learned their lessons about the electric fence
too. Kyle pulled himself back up on the tractor and maneuvered
the front loader over the hay feeder and deposited the round bale.
The dozen cattle—all Black Angus except for one whiteface—
stood in a row looking on in wonder. As soon as he backed the
tractor out of the way, the cattle clustered in a circle around the
feeder.

He winced as he got off the tractor again and walked back to
the feeder with a pitchfork. Shouldered the big black bodies aside.
Come on, guys. Give me some room to work here. He made space
for himself at the feeder and used the fork to help break apart
the bale. The cattle looked at him with big liquid eyes but kept
on chewing. The animals were learning to be afraid of strangers—
a stranger could be a veterinarian, which meant needles and
pinchers and things that burned. But they knew Kyle all their
lives, knew him as a friend. No one to fear. And he was comfortable around them, more comfortable with them than he was with
most people. Yet the day would come when he would help load
them into a truck, send them to the slaughterhouse. Would single
one out specifically to be held back, would continue to feed and
water it until the day he took it behind the barn and shot it

between the eyes. Would hoist it up with the same block and tackle he used to pull engines from the tractors and slit it open from balls to throat, spill its guts onto the blood-soaked earth. He would be the last thing the animal ever saw, its friend. It occurred to him that dealing with the animals wasn't that different than the dealings between people after all.

Six

When he saw Dan at the diner, he sat down next to him at the counter. As he usually did whenever he saw him, since they became friends through Julie. Since Kyle and Julie and Dan and his girlfriend Kathy would double-date, going to dances and concerts and clubs together, a whole new world for Kyle. A young world. Dan was busy talking to a couple of his friends. Kyle went ahead and motioned to the waitress that he wanted coffee.

When there was a lull in the conversation, Kyle said, "So, how's it going?"

Dan glanced at him and shrugged noncommittal, reset his camouflage cap on his head and turned back to the others. At first Kyle didn't think anything of it, figured Dan and his friends had something important to discuss. But Dan continued to ignore him. All three of them.

Kyle tried a couple more times. "How's Kathy doing? Say hello to her for me."

Nothing.

"Did you ever get your truck fixed? You were having trouble with the transmission."

It was as if Kyle were too far away for Dan to hear him. Finally he got it.

"You take care of yourself, Dan." Kyle took his coffee mug and carried it across the room. Three older men sat at their usual table against the windows. Regulars at this time of day. As Kyle approached, one of them pushed the empty chair toward him with his foot.

"Take a load off, young fellow," he said. "Have a seat at the Big Boy table."

Kyle sat down and looked at them. Nodded. Thinking, *So this is how it happens. This is when you start to know.*

Seven

Back in the barn, he turned off the engine, then sat for a while behind the wheel of the tractor. Listening to the metal tick cool. A loose board flapping in the wind. The creak of the rafters. Thinking about when this barn supported a hundred head. More, a few years. Back when the market was still good. Before he discovered he could make just as much with the gas-well royalties. Before keeping the farm going was more a labor of love—from a love of the labor— than as it was to earn a living. As he sat there he became aware of the whine of Sarah's Trailblazer coming up the hill from the house. Heard the door slam, her soft voice talking to the dogs. In a few minutes watched as she came down the length of the barn, Caleb and Jessie dancing around her as if they had discovered a great prize.

"So. You're just sitting alone here in the dark."

"'Pears so."

"You all done with the chores?"

"Finished up a little while ago. And now I'm just sitting."

"Appears so."

She grinned up at him. She was another one he had known all his life, though a few years younger, early fifties. Not like Julie. Not like Julie at all. The Mitchell Girl, as she was known. Had been to college, married and divorced, came back to run her family's nursery after her dad died. When she and Kyle started going out, folks in the area thought they were a natural. A perfect match. They even looked like they belonged together, same body type, tall and lean. She was wearing the buffalo plaid jacket she had appropriated from his closet a few months back. It looked like it was made for her. She looked like she was made for him too.

Eight

"I left the groceries down at the house. I thought I'd do a pork roast, you like the way I fix that. And later we could go over to the church. There's that fiftieth-anniversary party for the DeAngeleses. Or we could stay in and watch a movie." She flicked her thick wheat-colored hair, a look on her face that said she wasn't thinking of a movie if they stayed in.

Their normal Saturday. Weekend. Sunday morning they'd get up and go to church. Then to the Village Inn for brunch. In the afternoon they'd come back to the house, watch football or whatever was on till it was time to do chores. Either she'd help him, riding along with him on the Mule. Or she'd head home. The same as always, for the past year or so. Having found a comfortable routine. Essentially the same routine as his and Julie's. For that matter, the same as his and Ellie's. His way of life. He didn't know beforehand he was going to say it.

"Look, I think I'd like to be alone tonight."

"Are you okay?" She came toward him. "Is your side hurting again. . . ?"

He got down from the tractor. Stood before her, but not quite looking at her. "No, nothing like that. I just. . . ." He didn't know how to explain it. What there was to say.

She looked at him quizzically. Started to smile and then it went away. As if she understood better than he did. "Okay," she shrugged. Stuck her hands in the pockets of the buffalo jacket and started to turn away. Then turned back and gave him a kiss on the cheek. "Maybe you'll call me later."

"Yeah," he said. "Yeah, I'll give you a call."

She studied him one more time, then turned and walked back down the long aisle of the barn. Caleb and Jessie watching her go. But didn't go with her.

Nine

When he got back to the house, he fell asleep in his chair without meaning to. He woke suddenly, snuffling like he was choking. The house was cold and dark. It was evening, he had been asleep several hours. He stood up stiffly, turned on lights through the downstairs, lit a fire in the fireplace. He was trembling, he didn't know why. A dream? He couldn't lose the feeling that something big had happened. Something had passed him by.

In the kitchen he found the groceries Sarah brought on the counter. He put them away, remembering how happy she'd been when she talked about fixing him the pork roast. How her expression changed to something else when he told her he wanted to be alone. Caleb and Jessie had wakened when he did, followed him to the kitchen. He got them fresh food and water but they didn't touch it. They were watching him.

"You guys need to go out?" He took his barn coat from the peg near the door. The hounds followed him outside but instead of charging out across the yard they stayed with him. The night was brittle, the moonlit sky broken with clouds. He went down the steps and out across the yard toward the fields. From the woods came the call of an owl. Its mate on the opposite hill. A curl of smoke came from the sisters' triple-wide. Cars passed on the road at the top of the lane. An airliner vapor-trailed across the blue-black sky.

He needed to piss. He thought to make a design in the snow, an angel or figure eight like they did when they were kids. But it came out in squirts and dribbles. The knot in his side smiled. No, I haven't forgotten you. My new best friend. Life's companion. Till death do us part. I know you're not going anywhere. Caleb went over to sniff the steaming trail in the snow, but Jessie kept her eyes on Kyle.

So It Begins

UNCORRECTED PROOF: NOT FOR SALE

"The doctor said I had a mild heart attack. He said they're quite common, at our age. It's so strange because I never felt anything."

She sat across from him at the kitchen table. Not looking at him directly, only occasionally glancing over at him. Testing his reaction to her news. Her hands resting on the plasticized tablecloth. Her finger idly tracing the pattern of the red-and-white squares.

"There's nothing to do for it really. You know, I should lose a little weight. Try to watch what I eat. Cut out the greasy foods and brownies." She looked at him then. Her easy smile. "All the good things, you know?"

Her easy smile. That he had seen through the years of their life together. When he asked her to marry him after a dance at the grange. Standing at the altar of the United Presbyterian Church. When Billy, their first-born, took his first steps. After the funeral of their third child, Catherine, just a baby, when she took his arm on the way back to the car, looked up at him and told him, "So we go on."

"I don't think we should tell the kids," she said, looking again at her hand on the squares. "No need to press the panic button."

He took the last swallow of coffee and got up from the table. "Better get started. Before it gets any later."

He took his canvas coat from the hook and left the kitchen, out the back door. His daily late afternoon trek to the barn. It was dusk, the yard and fields in darkness, a line of what was left of the day tracing the shape of the hills beyond the road. From the barn he could hear the cows stirring, expecting him.

And he thought, So it begins. He always thought he would be the one to have problems first. His bad knees, cracked ankle. A lifetime of broken bones and chipped fingers and bad digestion. The jump in his breath the first sign of heart trouble. The dribble of urine the first sign of cancer. Not Sharon. Before entering the barn, he turned and looked back at the house. She stood in the window, backlit in the yellow glow of the kitchen, looking at him, or he supposed at the space in the darkness where she guessed he would be. He would give his life for her if he could, this woman. Trade places with her for the journey she was starting, the long slow final descent. But knew there was nothing in the world he could do for her now.

ONCE AND FOR ALL

He hadn't been in these woods for years. Maybe not since that summer with her. That summer after they graduated from high school. He would come up from his family's farm on one side of the hill, she would come up from her family's farm on the other. To walk through these woods together and talk about life. Their lives ahead. But not together.

He knew he should be wearing orange, but he kept the land posted, there better not be hunters. His footfalls crackled through the stillness, birds flying off ahead, small things skittering away through the dead leaves. Sunlight sprocketed down through the leaves overhead like searchlights for survivors. He remembered the birch tree was over toward the ravine.

"So, do you think you'll marry Jim?" he finally had the nerve to ask. That last day before she left to go to Penn State. Where the guy she dated went to school. Waited for her.

"What about you and Joann?" she asked. Stopped and looked at him. Not so much a question, he thought now, but a counter. An opening. Was that the moment, then?

He shifted the weight to his other shoulder. Moved on. Yes, the birch was ahead.

Unable to say it, he took his penknife and carved her name and Jim's in the trunk. Then she took the penknife and carved his and Joann's beneath it. Handed back the knife. To say Your turn? He folded the blade into the handle and put it in his pocket.

Sure enough, the names were still there. As he thought they would be. Though time had swollen them apart as the tree grew, thickened with age. Twenty years, where did they go? Back when he thought love was about the prettiest girl you could get. Not about best friends. Back before he learned that being naturals together was as good as it gets.

He heard about her from time to time. Heard she had five kids now. Lived in St. Louis. No reason to come back since her family died off. Her family's farm sold for a subdivision. No reason to write or call. And what would he say now, when he couldn't say it then? He fingered the carvings, the letters black with age and fungus in the white bark. Then hoisted the chainsaw off his shoulder, yanked the pull cord till the engine caught, and set to work to take the tree down. Once and for all.

So You Want to Drive a Tractor

First there are the pedals. Four or five of them, depending on the model and the age of the tractor. To the left is the clutch to engage (or disengage) the transmission while shifting gears. The next two pedals on the right are the brakes, one for the left rear wheel, the other for the right wheel. In most situations the driver presses both pedals to stop the tractor. In most situations. The independent brakes can help make sharp turns and control spinning in mud or soft soil. That is, if the two rear wheels are the driving wheels; if the tractor has four-wheel or front-wheel drive, there is a locking differential to even things up.

The pedal furthest to the right is the foot throttle. There is also a hand throttle, if the operator's feet are busy doing something else. Some row-crop tractors have a "de-accelerator" pedal that helps slow the engine during sharp turns at the end of a row. A fifth pedal just in front of the driver's seat operates the rear differential lock or diff-lock. Usually, a differential allows the outside wheel during a turn to revolve faster than the inside wheel; but in conditions where there is little traction, the differential could allow one wheel to slip, which would further reduce traction. The diff-lock overrides the differential, forcing both wheels to turn at the same speed and increase traction. Now, the driver has to remember to unlock the diff-lock before attempting a turn, for obvious reasons.

And these are just the pedals. The driver also must contend with the gear shift lever, clutch lever, power shaft shift lever, hydraulic control lever, radiator shutter control, hand throttle— oh yes, and the steering wheel. Keeping in mind that the machine is top-heavy and can tip over easily on the side of a hill or if one wheel slips into a ditch; or for that matter, with all that torque and oversized rear wheels, the farmer can pull the machine right over on top of himself. Most tractor-related deaths result from being run over or crushed by the tractor, becoming entangled in the moving parts of the tractor or its implements, accidents on roadways, and tractor rollovers. Most farm accidents are associated with tractors, and in the U.S. farming is the second-most dangerous occupation, right behind mining.

But I digress . . . you think that driving a tractor is fun, which it can be. Here, have a seat behind the wheel, the key goes in that slot there. . . .

A MATTER OF HYDRAULICS

"Did she drop the calf last night?" Adam said.

"Yeah, but I haven't had time to look at it yet," Jerry said from where he leaned inside the engine compartment of the tractor.

"The mother's on her feet," Ruth said. "That's a good sign."

They watched as the little boy ducked under the gate and headed across the field beside the barn. Through the herd of cows standing there waiting to be milked. The cows, a foot taller at the shoulders than the eight-year-old, watched him pass unconcerned.

"You don't have a choice," Ruth said. "This is your main tractor."

Jerry wiped the fluid from his hands. "Without the hydraulics, I can't get the hay to the feeder. I need to move the corn too. And they're saying rain by the end of the week."

Adam shouldered one cow out of the way and knelt where the calf was lying. Lifted a rear leg. "It's a girl," he called.

"How does she look?"

Adam pumped his shoulders a couple of times. "Okay, I guess."

"I can help with the milking," Ruth said.

"You've got enough with your job in town." Jerry looked at the engine, then back at his son in the field. "We need to get that work done on his teeth too."

"What's it going to take for the tractor?"

"I can't tell until I strip it down. Whether it's just the seals or something else."

By this time the calf's mother had come over to investigate. The boy stood and rubbed the mother's nose. Both the boy and the cow made a fuss over the calf.

"And we wanted to take that trip to Lancaster. You never get a vacation."

"Neither do you," Ruth said, rubbed his arm with the flat of her hand. "Don't worry, we'll figure it out somehow."

Now the boy was surrounded by half a dozen cows, all wanting their noses rubbed. Adam giggled as he talked to each one in turn, his friends. Jerry looked away, at the surrounding hills, the fields that had been in his family for generations. This place he loved so. When would the world stop pushing at him, always pushing at him?

O Good Shepherd

"What's all this?" Claire said.

In the bed of the pickup truck were half a dozen hundred-pound bags of sunflower and mixed birdseed, with a collection of birdfeeders, hooked poles to drive into the ground.

"While you were getting the herds in I went to the feed store," Mary said, busy spreading peanut butter on cakes of suet and birdseed bells.

The day was dark, the sky in folds of gray with the approaching snow, the first storm of the year. The wind a steady presence coming over the hills, the bare fields.

"But we have a couple feeders. . . ."

"We didn't have nearly enough. Not if the storm is as bad as they say. You said yourself it's going to be bad, that's why you wanted the herds closer to the barn."

She was wearing her father's green-and-black buffalo plaid wool shirt, the fedora her father used to wear to church and formal occasions converted to a barn hat. Claire looked over the fields at the distant woods. At the distant iron gate and fence around her family's burial ground, the few visible headstones glowing dully in the darkening afternoon.

"Mary, this isn't going to help him. You did all you could. Come in the house. . . ."

"No!" she snapped. Then softer, "No. It helps me. And it helps them."

She nodded to the black trees near the outbuildings. The branches filling with birds, cardinals, jays, finches, sparrows, interested in the proceedings. Crows kept a distant watch.

"You've got enough here to feed every bird in the county. Not to mention the squirrels and deer and woodchucks. . . ."

"Just because we don't feed them so we can kill them later like everything else we do around here. Don't you think they'd like to know there's one place they can count on?"

He looked at his wife of thirty-eight years. Among the lines that creased her face, the folds of skin drooped under her eyes, he could barely make out the girl he married. But he knew she was there. The first drops of sleet stung his face. He shook his head, took off his gloves, and began spreading peanut butter on a suet cake.

SLIP SLIDING AWAY

"I guess we won't be making this trip into town again after tonight," J.T. said.

"Careful," Larry said. "The nurse said he can still hear us. Here's to Al."

The two men raised their paper cups of Jack Danie'ls over the old man lying in the hospital bed. His hands folded on his chest rising and lowering fitfully with his labored breathing. The room quiet now since the nurses turned off the monitors and ventilator.

"He sure wasn't sick very long. I just saw him out mowing a couple weeks ago."

"He lived a long and full life. And it's a blessing to go like this."

"Definitely. With good friends by your side to see you off."

"Let's hope we're all this lucky."

Each man looked into his paper cup for a moment as if trying to read something there. They looked up at the nurse standing in the doorway.

"When did it happen?"

The two men looked quizzically at her.

"He's not breathing," she said, coming over to the bed and taking the stethoscope from around her neck. She listened to his chest for a moment and raised up and shrugged. "He's gone."

The two men got to their feet. After a few minutes Larry and the nurse started talking arrangements, the family members to be contacted, the funeral home to be notified. But J.T. continued to stare at the body. He had seen animals killed all his life, death and decay being part of farming as much as growing life. Had killed since he was a teenager, a coming-of-age like learning to drive or a first kiss. But that was different. Shooting a deer or a cow, wringing the neck of a chicken, slitting the throat of a pig— death was heralded with gurgling blood, the involuntary reflexes of the struggle to live. An event of a kind. Not this. This hideous nonevent. One minute Al was here; the next, a thing to be disposed of. Nothing to mark it even happened. That he was ever here at all. J.T.'s breath caught in his chest. He was more afraid than he had ever been in his life.

OLD FRIENDS

"Everything okay with it?" Charlie said, getting out of his pickup and coming over to where Ben was leaning into the side of the tractor.

"Just checking the filter. Been a lot of dust lately."

Charlie nodded. Ben finished tightening the wing nut and straightened up. Wiping his hands on a rag. Thinking, I have to ask. "How's Sally doing?"

"Not so good. I have to take her back up to Pittsburgh tomorrow for more tests. They think the cancer's back. We'll probably be up there a couple of days."

"You tell her Joyce and I are thinking of her."

"I will, I will," Charlie said. His hands in the pockets of his overalls under his barn coat. Not quite meeting Ben's eyes. And Ben thought, Just ask it, Charlie.

"You know, I usually ask the Phillips' boy, but he's out at the fair this week. . . ."

"You go ahead. I'll take care of your cows."

"I got the milk truck on Tuesday, you know. Usually gets to me little after midnight."

"I got him Wednesday. Usually 'bout the same time. I'll take care of it."

"You know, Ben, if there's ever anything. . . ."

"Don't think another thing about it. You just make sure Sally's okay."

"I will, I will." Charlie looked like there was something else to say, then lowered his head and went back to his pickup and bumped back across the field.

Ben watched him go. Thinking he had known the man all his life. Remembered the two of them as boys catching crawdads along the stream on the old Miller place. They hadn't talked in several years, not since they supposedly went halves harvesting the corn on Miller's place when the old man didn't want it. Only later Ben found out at the feed mill that Charlie shorted him on the split by a third. That was Charlie. And now he asked Ben to do his milking. With the milk trucks and all, he would be lucky if he got a few hours' sleep in the next three days. But there was never any question that he'd do it. That was what you did.

LIKE EVERYBODY ELSE

As they pulled out of the church parking lot, Darleen gave one last wave, then slid across the seat in the pickup against Charlie. Gripped his arm two-fisted as if holding on to a pole. She was so proud of him. That would show all the doubters, he had fit right in, he talked to everyone and even helped at the punch bowl. She was so proud.

"Fifty years of marriage," she said, referring to the couple honored at the party. "Someday they'll have a party like that for you and me, you know?" She snuggled closer.

"Yeah, I guess," Charlie said, after a while. Not looking at her.

"What's wrong, honey? I thought you had a good time."

He was quiet for a few minutes. Keeping his eyes on the road ahead. "I just wish you'd try a little harder, that's all."

"Try?" she almost laughed.

"You know. You could be nicer to me when other people are around. Like your friend Patty, the way she is with her husband. She's really attentive to him and everything. I just wish you could be more like that. That's all."

Darleen pushed away from him. Started to cry. Charlie pulled over to the shoulder.

"Now what's wrong? I was just saying."

He reached for her but she batted him away. Then she swatted at him half a dozen times, slapping his arm, trying for his face. "You bastard!" He hit her once backhanded across her cheek and mouth. Hard.

"I told you not to hit me. That's what you get."

He put the truck in gear and continued down the country road. She was beyond crying now, staring straight ahead herself now, her face stinging from the blow, her eyes pulling as if being sucked back into her skull. It wasn't that he hit her that broke her. It was the knowing that they would never be the same now. That her marriage was never going to be different. That they were going to be just like everybody else.

A CANCER

"Is cancer like a cold or something?"

"No, silly. Cancer is a disease. A cold is . . . something else. What makes you ask that?" Betsy pulled a tall stalk of grass from its sheath, chewed the end. The tassel flapping.

"I heard Daddy talking to Aunt Linda. He said Mommy has cancer."

Betsy and her younger sister Sally sat on the edge of the field, near the top of the lane, looking down into the shallow valley, at the house and the barns on the slope of the hill opposite. She pulled up her knees, pulled her skirt tight over them like twin pegs. Sally sat sidesaddle, legs tucked to the side, her bare feet peeking out from under her long skirt. Betsy had to be careful how to ask the little girl, so she didn't scare her.

"When did you hear him say that?"

"This morning, when they were in the kitchen. They didn't know I was there. I guess that's why Mommy didn't come back from the hospital. Does cancer make you look funny?"

"I think it can make you lose your hair. Why?"

"Because when Aunt Linda asked him, Daddy said it didn't look good." Sally started to cry. "I don't want Mommy to lose her hair. I love Mommy's hair. I love Mommy."

Betsy put her arm around Sally, pulled the little girl closer to her. "Mommy's going to be all right. I'm sure of it." She wasn't sure of it at all, of course. But that wasn't her main concern. Her father had told Aunt Linda and not her. So that was why Aunt Linda arrived late last evening, a surprise visit. Betsy thought she was number one in her father's heart. If something happened to her mother, it would be her job to take care of Daddy then, it would be just the three of them. She would be the mommy then. But if her father called Aunt Linda, he must be thinking that she would become the mommy.

Betsy held the younger girl at arm's length and looked into her face, wiped away the tears with her thumb. "Don't tell anyone that you heard them talking. But you need to keep listening in case they say anything else."

"Why?"

"Because Aunt Linda has come to take Daddy away. And we need to protect him, until Mommy comes back."

The little girl looked wide-eyed at her big sister. But Betsy knew Sally would do it. Sally would do anything she said. And she needed Sally right now. Now that she knew who her new enemy was.

A FUNERAL

The old pickup truck with the two men, each dressed in an ill-fitting black suit, a white shirt that needed ironed, a tie permanently crumpled, pulled into the parking lot behind the funeral home.

"Lot of people," Harlan said, taking it slow down a long row of cars and trucks.

"I guess they didn't know him the way we did," Ken said.

The two men looked at each other and grinned wryly.

"Yeah," Harlan said. "He could be a real bastard."

He found a spot at the end of the last row, beyond the gravel in the grass of the neighboring field. After Harlan turned off the engine, the engine ticking cool, the two men remained where they were, watching the others straggle toward the large brick home, threading between the parked vehicles, the women in their Sunday best, the men in their Sunday suits.

"Did he ever pay you the thousand he owed you?"

"Not a penny," Ken said, elbow resting out the open window. He spit into the field. "When I asked him about it one time, he claimed he already paid me back. When I asked him about it another time, he denied he ever borrowed it in the first place."

Harlan laughed a little silently, more like a burp or a twitch. "A real bastard."

"I mean, if he needed it, I never would have said anything. But I knew he had it."

"That heifer he sold me that time. He had to know it had tuberculosis when he sold it to me. And I should've known not to take his word it was okay. It died within three weeks."

"And he kept the money."

"And he kept the money."

"I don't know what we're doing here, you ask me."

"We certainly don't owe that fucker anything."

"I don't know what I could ever say to Janet either. What is there to say? You married a bastard, you're better off without him."

"I'm thinking we should just blow this off and go get drunk."

Ken nodded agreement. "What a bastard. He was even like that way back in school."

The two men continued to sit there for a while. Then, looking at each other, each one grimacing to the other, they got out of the pickup and started across the lot. Threading their way through the parked cars and trucks. Joining the others.

An Annunciation

I know what they're thinking, BJ thought as she stepped into the clinic waiting room. Hoopie. Farm girl. White trash. Most of the chairs along the walls were taken. Old people mostly, couples, one helping the other, an old man with a walker, an old woman in a wheelchair, though there were a couple young women BJ's age, which made it all the worse, one as if coming from work, in a smart outfit, a bright red wool coat, checking her iPhone for messages, another also well-dressed but with a little boy bouncing on her knee. BJ unzipped her brown plaid Walmart five-dollar special jacket, pulled off her sweatshirt hood, walked to the sliding glass window and signed her name and why she was there on a clipboard, then retraced her steps, back across the room—I know what they're thinking, What is she doing here?—taking one of the few empty seats, beside an old man, bent over, his hands resting on top of the cane between his legs, his head resting on his hands.

I wish I were dead, right about now. If it weren't for this I would.

The old man, his head still resting on his hands, turned to look at her. As if he heard her thinking. "You pregnant?"

"How did you know?" BJ said. Softly, in a whisper.

"Is he going to do the right thing?" he said quietly. No one else seemed to hear them.

"I don't know. He's gone. Working on a gas rig."

"Do you want it? Even if he doesn't come back?"

"More than anything."

"Then don't you mind what others think, daughter. You go with your heart."

Before she could say anything, the inside door opened and a nurse, in crisp sparkling whites with a blue sweater over her shoulders, checked the clipboard, then motioned to the old man. He pushed himself up, took a moment to gather himself, glanced back at BJ as if they shared a secret, then shuffled across the room, bent over as if under a great weight, and disappeared behind the door.

BJ was elated, she felt as if a lead overcoat had been lifted from her, at the same time she found that she was trembling uncontrollably, sweating, for a moment she was afraid she might pass out. She was grateful in a few minutes when the door opened and the nurse appeared again, checked her clipboard and called her name. As she stepped inside and the nurse closed the door behind her, BJ asked, "The old man, the one who just came in, is he going to be okay?"

"And what old man would that be?" the nurse said.

BUTCHERING DAY

"The boy needs to see this," Cole said to the reflection of his wife in the glass of the door. "You're making him soft. All he does is play on that computer."

"It's not all playing. He's learning things too."

"Well, he's old enough to learn this. How else will he be ready to take over the farm?"

"Over my dead body he'll take over the farm."

He turned to look at her. She stood across the kitchen, arms folded over her breasts.

"I mean it, Cole. I want more for him than just this."

"Or maybe what you mean is you want him to be more than just me."

Please say I got it wrong. Please say something to make it better. But his wife, the girl he'd been with since they rode the school bus together, the girl who seemed destined for him since the first time he saw her in grade school, standing there in the old twill work shirt and jeans and untied tennis shoes she wore around the house, only looked at him. Her face blank and impenetrable. Someone he didn't know. A woman he had never met.

As he closed the door behind him, he heard the shot from near the barn and he hurried up a little, not wanting to miss it, to be there with his son when he witnessed what they were doing, what they had to do if they wanted to eat that winter, to help him get through his first kill, to help him understand the seasons of life, life on a farm, thinking, All this time, I never had a clue, how she felt, I never knew she was that unhappy, unhappy with me, that she hated it so, hated me. . . . Close to the barn the cauldron of boiling water steamed in the chill clear morning light. The engine hoist they'd use for the butchering stood like a gallows, a guillotine.

When he reached the pen, Wilson had the ropes tied to the pig's rear legs and was starting to hoist the carcass, the boy helping to pull the chain on the winch. When he saw Cole, the boy's face lit up. "You should've seen it, Dad. Mr. Wilson dropped him with one shot, right through the eye. And now we have to hurry up and bleed it while the heart's still pumping."

The carcass hung upside down, splayed and ready to be gutted, the pink flesh of the underbelly still shivering occasionally; as the body swayed the nose pushed up little mounds of dirt. Wilson deftly slit the pig's throat, the blood spilling over the black earth.

"Oh wow," the boy said.

Cole turned away. He thought the steam from the cauldron, or maybe it was the cold air, was getting to his eyes.

INTRUDER

The wind pressed against the wall of the barn, he could feel it, hear it, the creaks of the old building in the night; it wasn't raining though they said it would, but it felt like it, acted like it.

"I know you're there," Virgil said into the darkness at the rear of the barn.

After a minute or so, a voice said, "I figured. That's why you got the pitchfork."

"You never know," Virgil said. "I could've brought a gun. Or the dogs."

"I guess." A man's voice. Maybe his own age, but Virgil couldn't tell any more about him. After another minute or so, Virgil took a few steps forward and placed a plastic sack on top of a barrel. Stepped back again.

"These here are sandwiches. And a couple bottles of water."

There was silence, only the sound of the wind outside, pressing. Fiddling with the loose-fitting door to the fields. I got to fix that, Virgil told himself, first thing tomorrow.

Finally, the voice said, "So. It's okay? Me being here and all."

"You can rest for a few hours. Catch your breath. But I want you gone by morning, first light. I'll be back then with the dogs."

"Thanks for not bringing them now."

Virgil half smiled to himself, blew a puff of air through his nose. The guy had no idea. Tear him apart. "If it was me, two, three in the morning, I'd start across the fields, head toward the lights, that would be Furnass. In the morning there's a bus into Pittsburgh, every hour around the quarter mark, you can get another bus from there. I'd go south into the mountains, West Virginia, Kentucky. Radio said they think you're headed to Canada."

"I didn't do it."

"I don't want to hear it."

"She had it coming, all right, but I—"

"I said I don't want to hear it!" Virgil said, almost shouting. Furious. Gripping the handle of the pitchfork hard. Then he got control of himself again. Said to no one in particular, "I don't want to know." He turned away, back toward the open doors, a black frame for the night, black on black, a setting for the house across the barnyard, the lights in the windows, the glow spent on the bare earth. Thinking, I know enough. Enough for a lifetime. Over his shoulder, he said, "Just be out of here. First light I'm bringing the dogs."

HORSES IN THE RAIN

The horses stood in the rain, in the darkness, ghosts, heads lowered as if weighted down with the rain, bedraggled, watching him cross the pasture. The pasture had turned into a bog, drainage always a problem here, his dad complained of it in his time; his footing was mushy, his feet already soaked in his leaky boots. He'd move the horses into the barn later, when he got back. It was time to dig out their blankets again too, that time of year; he had planned to get them new blankets this year, if things were good. Another thing that would have to wait. Make do with what they had. No help for it. He shifted the rifle in his arms as he stepped over the electric fence, cradled it again as he entered the woods, began to climb up the slope through the bare black trees.

The lights of the new house at the top of the hill glowed against what was left of the day, a band of gray on black, defining the crestline. The silhouette of the hills, now that the developers had cleared the land. Leveled the trees. He kept the rifle close to his body, shielding it as much as he could from the rain, the wet branches of the brush reaching for it. What did they say in Nam? Reach out and touch someone. Sniper humor. As he got closer to the house, he followed a shallow gully to the best spot, a small rise adjacent to the side of the house. With a clear view, a clear shot of the kitchen. He took up his familiar position just inside the treeline.

In the circle of the scope, in the bright lights of the kitchen, centered in the crosshairs, the woman moved around the center island. He adjusted the parallax, estimated for wind. He should have a spotter for all this; for that matter, he should be lying down, the rifle resting on its bipod; relaxing his muscles, monitoring his breath. *Find the natural point of aim at the natural respiratory pause.* The woman was tall, blond, still in the clothes she wore to her office. He didn't know her name but had come to think of her as Angela. Tonight they were having leftovers, warmed in the oven. Then her husband came in. Gave her a kiss on the cheek. Fixed their martinis. He shifted his position till the crosshairs covered the husband's face. The reporter asked, What do you feel when you kill another human being? Recoil, the sniper said.

He watched until the couple's dinner was ready and they had moved off to the dining room, toward the front of the house. Some nights he followed them, lined up his shot there too, but not tonight. He flipped the covers back on the scope, took the rifle from its resting place on the branch. Started back through the trees, back down the slope, his head bent against the rain. No, not tonight.

YOU NEVER KNOW

"That car comes by one more time I'm going to shoot it," Josh said.

"What car is that?" Terry said.

"That SUV. That's the third time it's come by here."

The two friends sat on the old canvas-covered glider on the front porch next door to the tavern, only a few feet from the road. They watched as the luxury foreign-made SUV went a few hundred yards up the road, past the post office and the boarded-up saddle shop, stopped and turned around and headed back their way.

"See?" Josh said. "Here they come again." He knew Terry was keeping an eye on him.

City people, he thought, out for a drive, lost or looking for some antique shop, but you never know, you had to be careful, the SUV pulling off the road onto the dirt shoulder, only a few feet from the two men, the woman in the passenger seat rolling down her window, all smiles, holding a piece of paper, a gauzy scarf over her hair, but you never know; there were four men in the old white Land Cruiser, passing by a second time, looking at his patrol, the man in the passenger seat all smiles, an old man, brown as tree bark, toothless, grinning at him saying something, Josh grinning back starting to raise his hand to wave when the men in the back seat opened fire with AK-47s and a grenade exploded somewhere near his feet and he heard Johnson scream and he reached for the Beretta M9 he carried in his jacket pocket but Terry had his arm, wouldn't let him move.

"I got this one, soldier," Terry said, with his easy grin.

He kept Josh's arm clamped to his side—Terry was stronger than Josh now, from the years of working the farm, Terry could never hold him like this back in high school, Josh could always pin him wrestling then, but not now, not since—talking easily to the woman, giving her directions to the right road, waving to her as they drove away. He waited several minutes before he relaxed his grip, took his hand away slowly. "How you doing?"

"I'm okay," Josh said. After a moment he added, "The head-ache's back."

"No surprise, huh? Take your meds?" When Josh nodded yes, Terry said, "Let's head on down to the pond. I hear there's a couple ducks looking for a handout."

Terry stood, stretched, moved to the end of the porch while Josh struggled to his feet, adjusted his Pirates cap over the missing section of skull, got his cane from behind the glider, dragging along slowly behind the other around the side of the building and down the backyard, Terry not watching, looking at the trees and a cat chasing a small white moth in the bushes, but there, just in case, Josh happy they were going to the pond, he liked the ducks.

ASHES, ASHES

It's what animals do, it's what they're for.

If she held the two-sided makeup mirror from her purse just right, the circle of light pierced the darkness under the porch of the old farmhouse, a small quivery spotlight that revealed the ball of orange and black and white fur, the old cat known as Puss, huddled into itself, barely breathing.

When Margaret got to the farm that morning—her weekly trip from Furnass to help her aged Aunt Martha since Uncle Harry died—she found pools of blood and feces in the garage, the smears on the door where the cat had tried to get out. Margaret found the old cat lying on the side porch, a favorite spot since it had been banished from the house, her aunt declaring the animal inconvenient since it stiffened with arthritis, was always in danger of having an accident. The cat had responded to Margaret's voice, purred as she rubbed its head; but when Margaret went to get a stool to sit on as she kept it company, the cat had dragged itself under the porch, as far to the back as it could get.

The beam of light divined the darkness. Margaret cooed to the cat, trying to comfort it by saying the things she told it while she cleaned the multiple cats' pans she kept for it in the garage, while the cat hung around her, head-butting her ankle, trying to reconstruct the affection it had known before: "Good kitty. Puss is a good kitty. Puss is a good girl." The light danced and quivered over the barely moving fur, the back end matted with dried feces and blood; Margaret tried to steady the compact with two hands.

Then abruptly the cat stood up and tried to walk but its hind legs were useless, the animal fell over onto a scrap of wood; on its side, the cat raised its head briefly, gave a silent call, and tucked back into itself. That's got to be the end, Margaret thought, but the ribs still continued to move, up and down, up and down.

After fifteen minutes or so, when the barely breathing cat didn't try to move again, Margaret got up from where she was lying, brushed the grass and dirt from her jeans, and went up the steps into the house. Her aunt was at the kitchen sink, a block of a woman wearing scrubs against the heat, peeling a hardboiled egg.

"Well, she's still alive," Margaret said to her back, "but it can't be much longer. If I could just get her out I could take her to a vet. I doubt he could do anything for her now, but at least he could put her out of her misery."

Her aunt, who had lived on farms all her life, who had sent cows and calves, goats and kids, sheep and lambs, pigs and piglets, to slaughter all her life, if she hadn't done the slaughtering herself, arranged the peeled egg in her hand so she could still manipulate her walker and, giving Margaret a blank look as she passed, a look of total unconcern and unawares and unknowing, as if she had no idea what Margaret was talking about, continued into the dining room to have her breakfast.

FRACKING

In the dark bedroom, the tree outside the window—an ancient sycamore, sprouted here a century earlier when its roots went in search of the nearby spring, its branches heavy with summer leaves, a swarm of black shifting shapes—was silhouetted by the lights of the new tank farm beyond the hill, the lights burning all night long, lighting the night sky replacing the stars, the moon.

Fred's dark shape passed across the window, back from the bathroom, his third trip so far this night. Prostate? Bladder like a crushed ball?

"I've decided," he said, sitting on the edge of the bed, his back blanking out the window before he swung his legs up under the sheet. "I'm going to take their offer."

"So they can drill here," she said to the ceiling.

"I see no reason why they shouldn't. And a lot of reasons why they should."

In her mind's eye she could see the animated video the gas company showed a group of them a few nights earlier at the grange hall. Picture the borehole drilled deep into the earth, then amazingly, curving horizontal into the layer of shale, a web of pipes reaching under their farm; the explosions of the perforating gun, the pumping of suspicious fluids into the fissures, then sucking the gas from the pockets where it hid for eons, bringing it to the surface.

"No matter the danger to the groundwater. Spilled chemicals in the streams."

"It should be okay. We have to take their word that they're going to do it right."

"And I'm sure they'll have a good reason when something goes wrong."

"Look, Rita, it's real simple. We can't grow enough crops to feed the cows. And with milk prices as they are, we don't make enough to buy feed. This way, we'll have money every month to support the place. And we don't have to keep the herd either. We'll have enough we can just live here, take things easy for once."

Harvesting checks, milking the system, she thought, but didn't say. She thought of her great-grandfather who started the farm, a hundred years ago. Her father working the fields, milking the cows into his eighties. She felt as if she owed something to somebody.

"Hey, look at it this way: maybe for once we can have a little fun. You know, like other people."

He reached for her, his hand sliding down her flank, toward the place she thought of as Down There; she turned away, rolled over away from him—the shadow of the leaves danced on the opposite wall, waving at her, mocking her—she was frantic to get away from him, couldn't stand the thought of him sticking it in her. Ever again. *What's wrong with me?*

THE BRIDGE TROLL

One

The feet were enormous. Each as long as a yardstick, bunions the size of basketballs, the toes gnarly. And heavy, rigid, every step took a concerted effort, lifting and placing each foot purposely, no wonder they needed a larger boy to do it, at least he could take some pride, some comfort in that. The hands were enormous too, the long fingers like tree branches, stiff, arthritic almost, bent into shape; he knew children sometimes would run up and want to be held and he could grip them in a way but he'd have to be careful, it would be easy hurt somebody, break an arm, poke out an eye.

And the head, huge, in keeping with the size of the feet and hands, ugly like them too, and though made from paper-mâché, heavy, top-heavy, if he wasn't careful when he bent forward he could topple over, or for that matter fall over backward, fall on top of some little kid and crush him like a bug—to say nothing of the smell inside the thing, the dried accumulated sweat of everyone who had ever worn the costume at the Covered Bridge Festival during the eighty- and ninety-degree days of early September, and something else too, a sour yeasty smell as if someone had thrown up in here, which he could understand it would be easy to do, he was already getting sick at his stomach, claustrophobic just standing here in the church tent—he felt trapped as if inside a great bell and he was the clapper.

He shifted his head inside the head so his face was as close as possible to the mesh window where he could see out, to try to catch a bit of fresh air. And saw himself in the full-length mirror Pastor Tom had brought along. Pink as scalded flesh, the Bridge Troll, a grotesque figure, in a tattered flannel shirt and too-short jeans, the perpetually open mouth with the tongue hanging out, the goofy look on his face, an exaggerated version of the popular conception of a hoopie, a hillbilly blown up to monster size, everything he hated about himself, where he grew up and lived, even his family, what he was in the eyes of the world. The face of Pastor Tom, puffy, bangs like his hair had been cut with a bowl, all smiles and good-fellowship, tilted in from the side of his mesh window.

"You look great, Adam, just great. You ready to put the fear of God into these sinners?"

Two

He made his way slowly along the arcade of tents, the booths with funnel cakes and hamburgers, raffles and drawings, Ron Mayer throwing pots like he always did year after year, Nello Monroe demonstrating his collection of old farm tools, the younger children riding the Slide for Life into a stack of hay bales, Sandy Gibbons onstage in front of rows of empty chairs except for a few old men, singing "Amazing Grace" and "Country Roads."

As he clomped along, the world moved shakily across his mesh window as if projected on a small fuzzy screen, the sounds of the festival far away, the heat of his breath blowing back in his face. The crowds along the arcade parted in front of him as he approached, like Pastor Tom talked about Moses parting the Red Sea, a miracle, people along the midway breaking into smiles, parents bending down to point him out to their little ones, mothers holding up babies to see him, for him to see them so he didn't step on them, fathers taking the hands of toddlers and telling them not to be afraid, that the monster wouldn't get them.

How did I ever get into this? he thought. Why did I let Pastor Tom talk me into it? I hate this.

A child—he couldn't see whether it was a boy or girl, couldn't tilt the head far enough to see—hit him like a guided missile, hugged him tight around the hips, its head hitting him squarely in the balls. He wondered if his groan was heard outside the head.

He reached down with the branch-like thumb, pried her free—a little girl, of course—held her at arm's length, the little girl giggling the whole time. Parents, grandparents, took photographs, a little boy joined the group, the Troll knee-deep in grinning children.

Then he saw her down the midway, among a group of girls from school, the high school in Furnass that he rode the bus to every weekday morning, the girls—all in their black cheerleader jackets, gold piping on the sleeves, a lick of flames bright red on the back—who never looked at him, passed him by in the halls as if he didn't exist, and to them he didn't, not a bus kid, a farm kid, his blue corduroy *Future Farmers of America* jacket a source of amusement for them—he had heard them, all right—her name was Jennifer, with her cream-like skin and red hair, her eyes the color of blueberries, the prettiest girl in school, who wouldn't look at him even in homeroom but was looking at him now, the girls giggling among themselves as he approached, clomping through the grass, the girls as he got closer all pretending to scream.

Three

The Bridge Troll waded into the group of girls, there must have been six or eight of them, the whole cheerleader squad, slumming for the day—why else would they be here?—come out from town and the well-to-do suburbs to laugh at the country folk, farmers, laugh at the food, the parade of tractors, the displays of supposed Appalachian handicrafts, the quaint country fair, tromped right into the midst of them, secure that they had no idea who he was inside the costume, the grotesque oversized head.

The girls screamed and laughed, circling around him, pretending to be afraid. He reached for them, grabbed at them, as if to pull them under the bridge, pull them into the water, hold them under, that's what the stories said about the Bridge Troll, that's what he would do if he could catch one, and the girls laughed and screamed around him, skipped around him, tempting him, daring him, pulling at the tatters of his shirt, at his patched jeans, avoiding his big pink feet.

"Watch out!" the girls screamed. "Run, run, it's the big bad Bridge Troll!"

Then she was in front of him, he saw her framed in the fuzzy mesh of the air hole, and he reached out with his branch-like fingers and caught her, one of the papier-mâché fingers under her breasts, another behind her across her ass, and he wouldn't let her go, he held her close to him as she lost the pretend fear and looked straight at the mesh window, looked into the darkness inside the mask, and she grinned and said, "I give up, you got me, Mr. Troll. Whoever you are."

And for a moment they looked at each other, through the screen, as close to her as he would ever be, her smile challenging, not unfriendly, just matter-of-fact, as if to say "Okay, so here I am. Now what are you going to do with me?" and he let her go, carefully so as not to hurt her, removed the pink branch-like finger from under her breasts, unwound the finger from behind her, and she danced free and joined her friends again, the girls running away down the arcade, giggling among themselves as if they knew a secret, and he stood there looking after them, the sounds of the outside world coming to him faintly through the darkness inside the head, a radio playing jangly music, people talking along the booths of the midway, a woman's voice warning, "He eats bad little children, you know," watched as Jennifer and her friends were swept along the gallery of gaily decorated tents, carried away into the swirls and eddies of the crowds, the crowds closing around them, absorbing them, lost to him forever.

PART TWO

THE HILL WIFE

One

The old man ran the blade of the shovel along the curb behind the stalls, scraping off the manure that didn't make it into the gutter—the raised floor of the stalls was the right length for most of his Holsteins, but a few of his girls were as short as a Jersey and their droppings hadn't quite made it into the trough— cleaned off the curb the length of the stalls on this side of the barn, having already done the other side, then pushed the mounds of shit—when he turned seventy a dozen or so years earlier he decided he was going to call it for what it was: shit; he remembered that Maddie was always squeamish to even call it manure, she always called it poo—back up the gutter, some of it still steaming in the morning chill, to where he had left the hopper of the litter carrier, shoveling the rich-smelling mounds into the hopper. Noah started to raise the hopper off the floor, pulling on the chain dangling down beside it, raising it shoulder-high where it would be easier to push along the overhead track, when he heard the voice among the metal creaks and rattles of the mechanism.

"You're still using that antiquated manure trolley. I would have thought it—or you—would give out long ago."

Two

He looked up over the end of the hopper, at the figure in the doorway of the barn, a black silhouette against the fields and the distant hills, a blank figure, but he needn't have bothered, he knew the voice. Noah went back to what he was doing, leaned his weight against the hopper, his face inches away from the load—it occurred to him too that the figure in the doorway called it poo as well, would think of the load as stinking, whereas he only thought of it smelling like cow shit, a smell that never offended him, that he grew up with, a smell he actually liked— moving the hopper slowly along the track toward the opening in the wall.

"I thought you'd probably show up around this time. If you were coming."

His son William stepped through the door, moving out of the way of the swinging hopper as it rounded a corner of the track.

"Have they come for her yet?"

Noah gave one last push to the hopper, sending it through the opening cut in the wall. Then he straightened up, trying not to show how much his back hurt him, wiping his forehead on the sleeve of his denim shirt. "No. Your mother's still up at the house."

"You mean your wife."

Three

Among the locals, the other farmers in the area, she was known as the Hill Wife, in the same way the place was known as Hill Farm, a shortened version of Thorn Tree Hill Farm, the name given when it was first settled in the mid-1860s, farmed by Noah's great-great-whatever-grandfather—the "greats" preceding "grandfather" too many for him to reckon or bother with now, he only knew there were a lot of them—the hill and maybe the farm too, eventually giving the name to the section of two-lane highway that was laid out in the early twentieth century, following the path of an Indian trail and later wagon road, on the way to Furnass, a wagon road running through the place being a convenience in the early years, though in time a band of concrete climbing up (or down) through the middle of the farm with speeding cars and trucks being quite another, nothing to be done about it by this time except learn to live with it. It was that ribbon of concrete that took young Noah away from the farm and into Furnass and then Pittsburgh when he was drafted into the Army during what was known as the Korean Conflict (at the time, never War); it was the same ribbon of concrete that brought him back from overseas to take over the farm when his father died suddenly, crushed when his tractor on a back slope of that self-same Thorn Tree Hill flipped on him; the same ribbon that took Noah away again in a few years though only for a week this time, to go to Kentucky to marry and bring back the girl he met in a restaurant outside of Fort Campbell when he was there for basic training and had corresponded with since, a case if there ever was one of, if not love at first sight, at least a shared recognition of the way things were bound to be.

Four

Her name was Maddie, a woman who fit perhaps too well the cliché descriptions of *string bean* and *a tall drink of water*, her Appalachian roots apparent in her gaunt serviceable frame, her gaunt face that showed determination and strength in equal measure with the generations of poverty that gave rise to those qualities, a girl who, the first time he saw her, a head taller than himself waiting tables in a soldier-filled diner, recognized—as she said later she did as well—that here was a person who was as much out of place away from hills and trees and planted fields and open skies as he was, even if the hills and trees and planted fields and open skies she knew and was away from were very different, in a different part of the country, than his were.

Noah's nature and predilections were so well-known among the other farmers around Furnass—men he had known all his life, most of whom he had gone to school with, or with their brothers and sisters—that when he brought Maddie home to what was now his farm they were so taken aback that any woman would try to take up with Noah—try to put up with his quirks and idiosyncrasies; the kid in the middle of the school bus or at the back of the class who never opened his mouth or volunteered an answer; who was always friendly enough if approached but generally went about his business without the encumbrance of friends or companions; who put up with going to school only because he had to, putting in his time only until he could get back to what really interested him, the only thing he cared about, his family's farm; who was basically so nondescript and unassuming that even in the senior class picture, with his image sitting right there on paper, people viewing the photograph rarely noticed him—that they could only refer to the woman he brought to live with him as the Hill Wife, meaning that the woman was now as much a part of and associated with this particular patch of earth as he was, the woman as much a part of the land as Noah.

Five

After pushing the litter carrier on its overhead track through the hole in the wall, Noah took his shovel again and walked past his son standing beside the doorway—he gave him a brief glance, but only a glance, a sidelong look up at the face of the man, William a head taller than his father, tall like his mother—and continued on outside. Noah hoped William would head on up to the house to see Maddie, but he trailed behind his father around to the side of the barn, stepping carefully in his tasseled loafers between the puddles of cow plop and mud from the recent rains. What does he want from me, Noah thought, why is he here? No, I know why he's here. Noah hooked the blade of the shovel on the edge of the carrier and dragged it the last few feet into position over the manure spreader—the shit wagon.

"Better watch yourself," Noah said, taking hold of the chain dangling from the carrier. "Sometimes it splashes." Don't want to get any on your fancy clothes. Thinking, What does he want me to say? No, I guess I know that already too.

Noah pulled two-handed on the chain—it took every bit of strength he had to make it look easy, he wasn't going to give William the satisfaction of seeing him struggle—overturning the hopper and dumping the contents into the wagon. None of it splashed but the smell was gag-worthy if you weren't used to it. William didn't seem to notice; he was busy side-stepping one of the barn cats—Popeye, Noah called him, from the time one of the cows kicked him in the head as a kitten and one of his eyeballs dangled out until Noah stuck it back in—who was trying to head-butt the man's fawn-colored pants. Who wears pants that color to a farm? Noah thought. Good enough for him.

"My offer still stands, Dad," William said, lifting one leg away and then the other, doing a kind of slow-motion Charleston away from the determined tuxedo cat. "I'll gladly pay to replace this carrier system with a modern gutter-cleaning rig. This hopper and track and all are real antiques, they should be in a museum somewhere. It would save you all this—Get away, damn it!"

William kicked at the cat, barely missing its head. The cat got the idea and sat down, out of range of the tasseled loafers, plotting. Noah studied his son, bemused at his struggle with the cat.

"You always did have problems with getting dirty, didn't you?" Noah said.

"Maybe I just thought there was too much dirt around here."

Six

"I wish you'd at least consider letting me replace that old litter carrier. Wouldn't a gutter-cleaning system make your life easier?"

Of course it would make my life easier, Noah thought. And it would make your life easier too, my son. Then maybe you wouldn't feel so guilty about leaving the farm. Leaving me to work it alone. You probably think I blame you for that, for wanting something more for yourself, but the fact is I don't. Never did. Maybe I didn't like it at first, maybe I was disappointed, but that doesn't mean I didn't and I don't understand it. For that matter I wish a lot of things were different. And I understand that your wanting to get away from here was about more than getting away from the dirt and filth. At least the kind you could wash off.

His face of eighty-some years was drawn vertical, the way a knot of tree roots would be if pulled from the ground, all vertical sinews, the eyes peering out as if from behind clods of dirt, murky though still bright and mischievous too, taking it all in despite or perhaps because of the gauze of years. His shoulders were rolled slightly, his body bent forward, as if always pushing against something or drawing something behind; his hands were curled into hooks, the fingers wrenched into that configuration by the arthritis that he swore wasn't going to get him, as if the years of holding on to the handles of rakes and pitchforks, scythes and the levers of tractors, had left their imprint, his hands ready to grip at any time, just place the tool in his proximity and it would fit on its own, without him even having to make an effort to grab it.

He took the push broom and swept the traces of dirt and manure into the troughs on either side of the milking aisle in preparation for hosing it all down. William stood at the door watching him, then came deeper into the barn.

"You won't even consider letting me help you financially, will you? You won't even consider it. Because you think you can do everything yourself. You always thought you could do everything yourself."

Noah stopped sweeping and looked at him. "I won't consider it because it's beside the point. I've already decided: I'm going to sell the milking herd."

William stopped, taken aback. "Are you selling the place?"

Noah went back to sweeping. Thinking, Maybe he's right, I guess I did always want to do everything myself. Because that's all I knew to do. And your problem was that you always took one thing to mean another.

Seven

"You should divide it into parcels, individual lots, rather than sell it as one piece. You'll get much more for it that way, anybody who bought the whole thing would divide it up anyway as a development. In fact, you could develop it yourself, make it into its own little subdivision, land values are going through the roof with this fracking business going on, people coming in with no place to build. My company would be happy to handle it for you, that's what we do, you know, maybe we could even work out an arrangement to take it off your hands. . . ."

Yes, he knew what his son did for a living, all right. He had mixed feelings about William's success. On the one hand his son had truly made something of himself, working his way up to a principal in a large real estate investment and development company. On the other hand, Noah had wondered at times if William was waiting for his father to die so he'd inherit a ready-made site. Now his son was implying that he'd buy the place from him. Well, that would be one way to get William back to the farm. Not that he wanted him back now—not now, not ever, actually—not that he would ever sell it to him, or anyone else, for that matter, as long as he was still able to work it. And as for inheriting it one day and developing it then, William was going to be disappointed in that too.

Eight

"You didn't hear me," Noah said, still sweeping though there was nothing left to sweep. "The same way you never hear me. I have no intentions of selling this place. I said I'm selling the milk herd."

"How will you support yourself? And . . . " though he didn't finish, only nodded in the direction of the house.

"You mean your mother."

"I mean your wife."

Noah took the broom and leaned it against the wall, busied himself straightening the harnesses and tack hanging on the wall though there hadn't been a horse on the property for thirty years. Thinking, And he still has trouble saying her name: Mother. Even though she's the one here he cares about, the one he's here to see. To see her before they take her away. So he thinks.

"I'm going to stock beef cattle. I can still do that. I won't have to milk them twice a day, try to fit those slippery milkers with these claws." He held up his hands with their bent and frozen fingers.

"Seems to me you always let a lot of things slip through your fingers," William said.

Nine

After William left, Noah went down the aisle of the barn and into the dark section behind the milk house, watching out the window at the figure of the middle-aged man who was his son picked his way carefully across the barnyard toward the house. He thinks he knows who he's going to go see; I hope he's ready for who he finds there. It's not pretty, it's not his mother. Or my wife, as William would be quick to point out. The boy was never good at handling the unexpected, or seeing what might come his way beforehand, got himself into all kinds of trouble because of it.

The time I was out in the fields and William—what was he, eight? ten?—got it into his head to turn the litter carrier into a roller coaster, stood on a milking stool to climb aboard the up-turned hopper, then used a shovel against the rafters to push himself along, gaining speed as he traveled through the barn and around the curve and out the window till he came to the end of the line above the manure spreader. Except the dead man latched on him and he was stranded there a few feet above the stinking load and had to wait there hours, the inverted hopper threatening to right itself or buck himself off into the manure every time he tried to shift his weight, until I came in from the fields and found him there, laughing my head off at his predicament which he didn't appreciate one bit or when I pretended I was going to leave him there overnight. Did his hatred of dirt start then? When he was younger, he would follow me out to the barn every morning, stay with me all day through the chores, the milk truck drivers called him my shadow, Little Noah, even wore the same kind of overalls I did, a smaller version of a John Deere cap. If that was the kind of dirt he was referring to. No wonder he wants to get rid of that old litter carrier now. As if I didn't.

Ten

In the corner, the calves stirred in the darkness. Three of them, heifers-in-waiting. He had always kept the calves here, his father too, as soon as they were taken from their mothers within twelve hours after birth, the mothers apparently uncaring about the separation though lately Noah wondered what the calves thought about it, kept in the dark here on the theory of what the calves couldn't see they couldn't miss, the new practice being to keep them in hutches like large dogs out in the light, something he wished he could do but something that was beside the point now. Another reason he would be glad to raise beef cattle where the calves were kept with their mothers, allowed to run free—that is until at some point later in their life they were loaded on a truck and taken away to be slaughtered. Life on a farm. Life as it is, he thought, just depends on what does the killing.

Eleven

W as it five years since he'd been to the farm? In the house? Seven? It must be fifteen, maybe twenty since he'd been in the barn. You get busy, he told himself, but knew that was no excuse, Pittsburgh, fifteen miles away, seeming lifetimes away. William headed across the barnyard, choosing his way carefully as if crossing a minefield, trying not to step in anything that would soil his loafers. He had expected the dirt of the place—it was a farm after all—but he was surprised at how run-down the place seemed, niggardly, mean even. Poor. The only reason he was here now was the doctor's office had called the backup number when they couldn't reach his father—of course they couldn't, William thought, the old man would be out in the barn or the fields, where he always was—and learned of the plan to put his mother in a home. Well, he was going to put a stop to that idea. Some long-harbored revenge on his father's part, he surmised. Put her away to get back for past hurts and offenses. He wasn't going to let the old man get away with it.

Twelve

A dozen barn cats sat in the tall grass close to the house, watched him pass, bearing witness. Funny, he automatically headed around to the front of the house, to the front door, like a visitor, rather than a son returning home, rather than to the back door that would lead him directly into the kitchen, the way he would have when he lived here. He had grown up playing in this grass, among the trunks of these trees, up and down these front steps; now his feet barely fit the narrow treads, built for the smaller feet of smaller people who built this house more than a hundred years earlier; from these warped floorboards, these blistered and peeling balustrades he had held off assaults of Indian war parties coming across the fields, Jeb Stuart's cavalry coming up the road. He was not surprised when the doorknob turned in his hand, the front door opening unopposed. But he was not prepared for stepping back into time, like a stage set for a drama that had played out countless times but only in the farther reaches of his mind. The rooms were kept immaculate, spotless, and unchanged for decades, every chair, antimacassar, knick-knack, cushion, lampshade, in place in the dusty half-light of the closed drapes. The house deathly silent. After touring the rooms, he thought his mother must be upstairs, but then saw her in a corner of the living room, sitting in a rocking chair, dressed in a white nightgown, her long white hair down around her shoulders, in her bare feet, having watched him pass by a couple of times. "Oh, there you are. How are you?"

She appeared collapsed in upon herself, as if the air and maybe the water too had been sucked from her body, leaving a husk of who she was before. She smiled like she knew something he didn't.

"Have you seen Billie? Dad said he would probably turn up here today, but I haven't seen him."

Thirteen

"It's me. Billie."

"Do you know Billie? He's my son. He lives in Pittsburgh. Is he here yet?"

Her skin was waxy, hideously smooth where it might have been wrinkled with age, as if she had been shrink-wrapped in semi-opaque plastic so he could see the webs of veins and arteries underneath. She was looking at something across the room behind him as she spoke; William turned to see what it might be, but there was only the china closet in the corner, a painting of a peasant girl herding geese on the wall. She rolled something in her fingertips but he couldn't tell what it was.

"He's a very important man in Pittsburgh. He builds shopping centers, you know, malls. And houses, acres and acres of houses, nice places for people to live in. He was always like that, when he was a little boy he'd use Jell-O and pudding boxes to lay out a little town for himself, with paper streets and everything. That was Billie. Always concerned with how people live. Of course, when they don't live up to the way he wants them to, well. . . ." She looked at William for the first time. "He's a very busy man so he can't come to see us very often."

He was confused; he had no idea that she was like this. Why didn't his father say something about her condition? Afraid William might try to stop him from putting her in a home?

"I'm sure he'd come more often if he could."

"I don't think so. Billie's mad at us." She worried the brown ball between her fingers, staining her fingertips.

"Oh, I don't know. . . ."

"I do. A mother knows these things. The thing is, he's not even sure why. He thinks he's mad at his father because I left that time. Ran away and left him. As if his father could have kept me from going. But you can't tell Billie anything, Billie always thinks he knows what's right."

What she was saying barely sunk in; he realized what she was rubbing between her fingers was feces. Human feces. "Where did you get that?"

His mother looked at the brown ball between her thumb and forefinger and shrugged. "On the floor. Your father thinks I've been dropping them around, but that's just silly. If you want some for yourself, there's a whole string of them over there in the corner."

He gagged into the elbow of his shirtsleeve.

Fourteen

He told himself that it was no different than cleaning up a baby, little Lori or David, when they dirtied their diapers; only this wasn't a diaper that could be dumped in the trash, this was his mother's fingers, and this was his mother. Then he remembered he hated cleaning up the babies too, whenever possible he ducked out of it, let Susan his wife do it.

But he did it anyway—as he kept reminding himself, it is your mother—got soapy paper towels from the kitchen and cleaned her hands as best he could, then got more paper towels and dispensed with the ball of feces, picked up the string of light brown turds across the room. He walked through the downstairs but didn't find any more, his father must have picked up any others.

He got her settled again, turned on the television—it was preset, muted, to a cartoon channel, Tom chasing Jerry through a cartoon version of the room he was standing in—then retreated back outside, stood on the porch. He had no idea that she was like this. That she had had accidents before meant that someone had cleaned her up before—must have been his father from what she said. Cow shit, wife shit—the man was surrounded by it, though William didn't think it was at all funny. He no longer thought his father had a revenge motive for putting his mother in a home; in fact it seemed a kindness to get her someplace with professional care. Someplace that at least had diapers for her.

Why didn't his father tell him she was this bad? But he knew the answer; it wasn't as if he and his father had any communication these days—about anything. He wondered if his father had told him beforehand, alerted William to her condition, if he would have come sooner. He would like to think so, but he knew he couldn't be sure. As his mother said, he was a very busy man.

Fifteen

He stood on the porch, looking off at the fields. In the distance he could see the tractor and manure spreader making their way back and forth across the slope of a hill. He was standing here that day when he was eight years old and he watched her leave in a car with. . . . His father was out in the fields as usual, the tractor and plow leaving their scars on the distant hills while the departing car dug furrows in the boy's heart where the hatred would grow. His mother was right, he had never forgiven his father for not preventing her from leaving, his father had always cared more for his cows, his girls as he called them, than he had for anyone else, much less his son; but then his father always could be counted on to make the wrong choice, the questionable investment, plant the wrong crop at the wrong time or sell at the wrong price. For that matter, he couldn't stand his father's nose hair, the gray chest hair sprouting from the neck of his work shirt like steel wool, his annoying little cough—the wrongs tumbled out; William wanted to leave, run as fast as he could out of there, all the bad feelings for the farm and his family came crashing back. But he was here now, he would stick it out until they came to take his mother away. Once and for all. He sat on the porch swing and glided slowly back and forth, back and forth.

Sixteen

The quiet of the house settled around her like a familiar shawl. Was somebody just here? She couldn't remember though it seemed like it. Maybe it was that nice man who came sometimes to feed her, help her to the bathroom, lay beside her in bed. She felt comfortable around him, he never tried anything with her, not like all those other men. Her attention was drawn momentarily to the luminous screen across the room where a cartoon cat chased a cartoon mouse through a cartoon house. All very funny, until you saw the real thing, which wasn't funny at all. She settled back in her chair and closed her eyes, not because she was sleepy but because she wanted to shut out the world for a while, what had reality ever done for her, it was all too demanding, too relentless.

My son, my son, what have you done?

That's right, it was William who was just here; she felt bad, Noah said the boy might turn up today but she didn't believe him, another story to keep her pacified, she hadn't fixed her hair or anything. Oh well, William would just have to take her as she was. That's all she had ever asked of William, of her husband, of any of them. Though apparently it was too much.

Seventeen

She remembered that the nice man who came to help her was her husband, Noah. He was always coming to her—though there was a time she recalled when it felt more as if he came at her—since the time she first met him. Whether she wanted him to or not. He came to her in the diner, outside of Fort Campbell, and kept coming back even before she discovered she wanted him to, came back to her in letters from Korea and after his discharge; then there he was again in person, ready to take her at her word, ready to take her with him, and she ended up here, a farm wife, with a little boy—oh, it was nice enough, the fields and the woods, the century-old house and the big fluffy clouds coming over the hills, a kind of substitute, a replacement for the home she lost in Kentucky. All ready-made for a life here, coming to her, coming at her. The neighbors from neighboring farms, the men at the feed store, the families at the grange, the good folk at the Presbyterian Church, all who had known him since a child, knew his family for generations. He came after her too, that time when she went away. As if he knew that she didn't really want to be away though she couldn't have said at the time what it was she had fled to, couldn't have said what she had fled to get away from. She couldn't say now, though she had an idea. Better to keep such things to yourself. Not for the nice man's sake, not even for the sake of the boy, what was his name? For her sake only. If she was going to stay on here.

My husband, my husband, what have we done?

Eighteen

When Noah got to the edge of the field, he stopped the tractor, set the brake and left it idling, and sat there for a moment, figuring: it had rained earlier in the week, the manure was wetter than usual, so he should figure 61 or 62 pounds per cubic feet, rather than 55 pounds when it was dry. Let's see: there were 43,560 square feet to an acre, 2,000 pounds per ton . . . he ran the calibrations in his head, then got down from the tractor and with the controls on the back of the spreader adjusted the speed of the conveyer pushing the manure toward the rear of the box, the speed of the shredders and beater paddles to spread the manure. Then he took his seat again at the wheel of the tractor, released the brake, put the machine in gear and lurched forward to start his journey back and forth, back and forth across the field.

He bumped along, the fine brown powder spewing out behind him, the occasional large chunks flying up like shrapnel. In the distance he could see his house sitting among the trees. He wondered if William was still there, and what his reaction was to seeing his mother. It was undoubtedly a shock, but William would never have believed her condition unless he saw it for himself—he knew that much about his son. He had intended to call William to let him know what was going on—he was sure his son would never believe that either—but the errant doctor's call took care of that for him. It was probably just as well, the information coming from the doctor's office would give credence to it, authority. He wasn't sure that William would believe anything he said at this point. He wondered when that changed, but of course he knew well enough.

Nineteen

He wondered, if William was still there, if he was watching the tractor crawl toy-like over the faraway fields, the same way Noah was watching the miniature house among the distant trees. All in the eyes of the beholder. As a little boy, William was the beholder of everything, Noah remembered, his shadow—no, the watcher in the shadows, why was that? Was he trying to learn from his father, or did he already know something about him? Ironic, that this would be the chore I'm doing, the day he is here. He was with me the day I bought this spreader, like he always was when I went into town, sitting there so proud in the pickup beside his dad. Unfortunately, she was there that day too; Maddie never went with me on errands, but she did that day, the three of us together, bumps on a log across the bench seat in the cab, our little family. Out to buy a new piece of equipment, an occasion, an event, a milestone in the life of the farm. I guess, in all the wrong ways, it was.

Twenty

"Well, look who came down from the hills. The Hill Farm, ha ha. Get it?"

Noah had known Charlie Holmes since grade school in Furnass, the class president in senior high, voted Most Likely to Succeed, who took off for the bright lights of nearby Pittsburgh as soon as they graduated, bouncing around between various car dealers until he landed back in Furnass at the John Deere dealership. Apparently he was able to parlay the fact that he grew up in the proximity of farms, if not actually on one—his family lived in one of the first subdivisions built on former farmland after World War Two in the rolling hills outside of town, his father a machinist at Furnass Screw & Bolt—to convince the dealership that he was qualified to sell tractors, even though he had never even ridden on one before in his life. An impressive if questionable act of salesmanship right there. Still, the few times Noah had seen him when he came to the dealership for parts, Charlie had always been friendly, salesman-friendly. They shook hands now but it was obvious Charlie was more interested in Maddie.

"And this is your family. What's this young man's name?" he asked Maddie, cupping his hand over eight-year-old William's head, palming it like a softball. William ducked away, and when that didn't remove the man's hand, reached up and brushed it aside. Charlie Holmes laughed, adjusted his tie.

Twenty-one

"And this is the lady folks call the Hill Wife I've heard so much about over the years." Charlie took Maddie's hand in two of his and looked directly into her eyes. "I can see for myself why she's been the subject of so much conversation, and speculation I might add. No wonder Noah's kept you tucked away all this time."

"What is the speculation about me?" Maddie said. Her Kentucky drawl reappearing, the first time in years. Making no effort to remove her hand.

"The speculation is what a beautiful woman like you is doing with a guy like this," Charlie nodded in Noah's direction.

"You're a flatterer, that's what you are," Mattie said.

"I just calls 'em the way I sees 'em," Charlie said.

"You sellin' something here besides bullshit, Charlie?" Noah said. He said it like a joke, offhandedly, his Noah smile on his face, but all three of the adults present got the message.

"Why sure, Noah, what did you have in mind? You finally going to replace that old tractor of yours? You've been holding that together with baling wire for years now."

"Actually, I'm looking for a new spreader. . . ."

Charlie hooted, sharing the joke with Maddie. "Wow, talk about spreading the bullshit around. Ha ha. Get it?"

Twenty-two

He turned around on the tractor seat to check the spray coming out of the rear of the spreader, then continued on to the end of this pass and started back the other direction. The irony being that Charlie, in spite of anything else that could be said about that day, sold him a really good piece of machinery, the same spreader he was using now, fifty-some years later. He went to the dealership that day with a low-end model in mind—he didn't need anything fancy, not for his small operation—but Charlie talked him into, maybe shamed him into was more like it, a heavy-duty, top-of-the-line John Deere, three-hundred-bushel capacity, the works; Noah made a futile attempt to hold out against the power-take-off Charlie insisted he needed, but that was about it.

"You won't regret it," Charlie said, standing close beside Maddie, addressing his comments to her. "You get what you pay for in this world."

"Not always," Maddie said. "Sometimes you get more than you bargained for."

"Better than getting less than you bargained for," Charlie said.

"Oh, I can certainly attest to that."

"I don't know, Maddie," Charlie said. "You strike me as a woman who never settled for second best. In anything."

"Sometimes you don't have a choice."

"You always have a choice," Charlie said, tilting his head to her, looking at her under his eyebrows.

"When you two are through with all your double-talk, maybe we can get back to selling me a spreader."

"That's what we always loved about you, Noah. Down-to-earth, no-nonsense, a let's-get-on-with-it kind of guy." Charlie reached for William's head again, but the boy successfully dodged away. "Let me tell you, son—"

"I'm not your son," William said.

The three adults laughed; Maddie held the boy against her leg, more to keep him from saying anything else, it occurred to Noah later, than to claim him for their own.

"The boy has thoughts of his own," Charlie said, smoothing his tie. "Ha ha."

Twenty-three

That evening back on the farm, as Noah was leaving the barn after finishing the milking, he found William standing in the half-light outside the door, waiting for him. Across the barnyard, the lights of the house glowed yellow in the dusk.

"Why did you let him talk to you like that, Dad?" the boy said. "Make fun of you like that?"

"Who, Charlie? He didn't mean anything, he was always like that."

He started to move the boy along toward the house, but the boy stood rooted.

"Then why'd you let him talk to Mom like that?"

Twenty-four

Thinking back later, he supposed he should have been aware of what was going on, recognized the signs. Was his lack of awareness because he was too preoccupied with the farm? But what was new about that, he was always preoccupied with the farm—cows getting sick, feed to be measured out and distributed, machinery breaking down. It was worse to consider that he had been aware of what was going on, did recognize the signs, and didn't care. No, it wasn't that he didn't care—he was not one to think about love, what it was, if he felt it—but he could see that he took his feelings for Maddie for granted, and more than that, took for granted her feelings for him. Of course the bond between them was tight and secure, what else would it be?

There was something else too, something else he was more reluctant to admit about himself, admit that he could think such a thing: It was flattering that Charlie Holmes might be attracted to anything that was his; in high school Noah coveted (it was when he learned firsthand the meaning of that biblical word) Charlie Holmes' nice clothes, the fancy car he drove (true: it was his family's Oldsmobile; but Charlie drove it to school dances on Friday, up and down the main street of Furnass in the evenings), the girls who hung around him. There was Charlie's easy way of talking to people; yes, even his good looks (it was gratifying that Charlie now had a muffin roll over the top of his pants, the flushed face of a heavy drinker; why would any woman, much less Maddie, be attracted to the guy?). Charlie always had nicer things than the farm kids, and made a point to let everyone on the bus know that, while the other kids headed home to do chores around their families' farms, he was going home to pore over the latest issue of *Hot Rod* and other teen-oriented magazines so he'd be aware of the latest trends, the latest fashions. So he'd be ahead of everybody else.

Charlie Holmes. Maddie. After all the years, it still seemed impossible.

He got to the end of the pass, made his loop and started back the other way.

Twenty-five

What was it then, a kind of pride? A character, personality flaw? That he was stupid? A fool? He wondered all over again, for the hundredth, the thousandth time. At the time he thought it a bit out of the ordinary that Charlie showed up—driving a top-down convertible—when the spreader was delivered, but Noah decided it must be an extra measure of service for an old friend, or, more likely, that Charlie was following up on a lead that he hoped would result in the sale of a new tractor.

He thought it peculiar when, a few weeks later in the midst of plowing his south forty, Charlie came walking across the field, slipping and sidestepping in the fresh earth, but coming on   regardless, his wide-faced Charlie grin on his face, his top-down convertible parked along the road.

"Hey Noah, how's it going?"

"Okay, I guess. What are you doing out this way?"

"I was in the area on a call and thought I'd stop by. That new spreader doing the job for you?"

They chatted about sticky control levers and pattern adjustments for a few minutes, until Noah said, "Well, I better get back at it," and Charlie said, "Yeah, I've got a few more calls to make before I get back to civilization," and off he went again, back to his car, driving off over the hill, giving a couple toots and a wave from where the roof should be. Noah put the tractor in gear and continued down the row, thinking no more about it.

Twenty-six

Thinking no more about it, until a week or so later when he came back from a trip into town to the feed mill and found Charlie's convertible, top up this time, parked beside the house, and Charlie sitting in his kitchen having coffee with Maddie. Charlie laughed, made a joke about compromising situations, said he was just leaving anyway, and was gone a few minutes later.

"What was that all about?" Noah asked Maddie as he watched the white car turn around in the barnyard, Charlie almost backing into a stump beside the service shed, before speeding off, gravel pinging down the highway.

"It was nothing, Noah. Nothing at all," Maddie said, redding the table of the coffee cups, keeping her back to him as she worked at the sink.

And maybe he would have gone on taking Maddie's word that it was nothing, nothing at all when it came to Charlie Holmes. But as Noah started out the screen door he saw William standing in the doorway to the dining room. Just standing there, watching him.

Twenty-seven

The boy would stand watching him, never saying anything—
never having to say anything—when Noah would come in from
the fields or the barn and find their station wagon gone, Maddie
away somewhere, when she returned giving some vague excuse
about having to run an errand or do a bit of shopping, though
there were never any packages with her, nothing to show for it.
The boy would stand there and watch him when the overnights
started, Maddie gone when Noah returned to the house from the
evening milking and home again when he returned from milking
the next morning, his wife never saying where she had gone and
Noah never asking—she didn't need to say; he didn't need to
ask—the boy standing silent, as if on a vigil, as the man and
woman met each other in the kitchen, neither one saying a word
as they went about fixing breakfast, getting William ready for
school. He stood there watching when the single overnights
turned into two- and three-day disappearances, long weekends
that began midday Fridays and extended into Monday, then
Tuesday, Wednesday.

The boy was standing on the front porch the day Noah
returned from running over to Ohio to pick up a part for the
tractor, the closest John Deere dealership now that he refused to
go to the one in Furnass. This time their station wagon was still
in the yard.

Twenty-eight

He climbed out of the pickup and approached the front steps, looking up at the boy standing beside the post. "Is she gone?"

The boy nodded. And then spoke to him, the first time he had said more than a cursory "Yes sir," "No sir," in weeks. "With that guy, Charlie."

"Of course."

"He said last week he wants me to call him Uncle Charlie."

"You can if you want to."

"He said that after I said I wouldn't call him Dad."

So it had come to that. Noah thought for a moment. "Well, you could call him that too, if you think it's appropriate." When the boy seemed puzzled by the big word, Noah said, "If you think the name fits."

"I don't even know if it fits to call you Dad anymore."

"Why wouldn't it? No matter what happens, I'm still your father."

But the boy didn't reply. He turned and went into the house. Noah might have followed him and pursued the topic but there was milking to be done, a round bale to be brought in from the field and put in the feeder, the milk house needed to be cleaned.

Twenty-nine

William didn't explain what he meant when he said he didn't know if it still fit to call him Dad until years later, until after he'd returned from Penn State and announced that he wasn't coming back to work the farm, that without telling his parents he had changed his major from agricultural to business and had accepted a position with a real estate developer in Pittsburgh.

"Are you still that mad at me? After all these years?" Noah said. They were on the front porch of the house, on what would be one of William's few trips back to the farm over the years, the visits becoming increasingly rare as his life and career in Pittsburgh flourished and he withdrew further and further from what he was afraid would be perceived as humble beginnings, even this visit more of just a stopover on his way from the university to his new job, not even waiting to attend his graduation ceremony. Noah wondered if the boy left his car running in the barnyard.

"My decisions had nothing to do with you. It's about having talents for doing other things besides milking cows and shoveling manure the rest of my life. And don't worry, I'll pay back what you spent on my education. I start out making more in one month than you make in a year. Good-bye, Noah." William ducked his head, as if he knew the import of his words, and headed down the steps.

Thirty

"Noah," he repeated after him. "Not Dad. Or even Father. You never did tell me why."

William stopped, considering what he wanted to say, then seemed to make a decision. "Okay, I'll tell you, if that's what you want. It's because when Mom left you never did a thing to stop her, you just let her go. And I figured if you didn't care anymore than that about your wife, you probably didn't care anymore than that about your son."

The question had haunted Noah for so long he wasn't prepared for it to be answered. What could he say? He wasn't prepared for a discussion like this, he didn't have the language, it wasn't in his makeup to discuss emotions, he only knew to act on them. He could have never described his feelings for Maddie, they seemed self-explanatory to him; and as for William, anything he might think to say—such as "I love you, son"—sounded trite and ridiculous and, more than that, beside the point. He stood there expressionless, unblinking, knowing he would endlessly regret that he had nothing he could say.

"You see?" William said, pulled a face, and continued to his car. Noah took some consolation that William hadn't left it running, had to start it.

Thirty-one

William sat on the swing on the front porch, one foot extended, one foot dragging as he swung slowly back and forth, accompanied by the squeaks of the metal chains, the creaks of the ceiling boards pulled by the shifting load, watching the tractor and spreader with his father—he guessed he should call him that after all this time, all that had happened, that was only right— crawling bug-like over the slope of the distant field. Thinking that the situation certainly seemed a whole lot clearer to him before he got here. He had jumped to the conclusion that his father was sticking his mother in a home to get back at her for past trans- gressions, but his opinion changed—radically—after seeing her condition for himself. An irony that wasn't lost on him. It was uncomfortably similar to his condemnation of his father in the past for letting his mother run off, an opinion that changed— radically—after he had the experience of being the one to run out on a marriage.

Growing up, he hadn't understood why his father hadn't fought to keep his wife; now he wondered what it was that drove his mother to leave. And for a guy like Charlie Holmes, for heaven's sake. Sheer boredom? His father was a man of routine, the farm, the cows, took precedence over anything else. He couldn't remember ever taking an overnight trip with his parents, much less a vacation. His father would say he couldn't leave be- cause of the milking, but there were in fact neighbors who would have done it for a few days, the same way his father milked for them when they went away. For that matter he couldn't remember sitting down as a family to watch TV, going to a movie together, couldn't remember his father and mother talking about anything except the farm, which heifers were ready for breeding, what changes to make to the feed to up the butterfat. He couldn't remember his parents ever sharing a laugh together.

From the barn came the cry of a rooster crowing. At midday? That was like his father too—have a rooster that crowed at the wrong hour, and keep the bird anyway. Not even consider it amusing or out of the ordinary. Simply accept it, that he had a quirky rooster, and keep it regardless. William looked out over the fields; he could no longer see the tractor though he could hear it, echoing through the hills, hidden somewhere.

Thirty-two

Back and forth, back and forth. He noticed there were grooves worn in the floorboards of the porch, from people in the swing dragging their feet. He was following well-worn paths.

It was so easy to know what was right when you were eight and twelve and a teenager, a recent graduate from college. You'd think the world and its choices would become even clearer, more defined, the older you got, but the opposite was true. The world was truly murky at fifty-two.

He could hear the tractor among the hills but still couldn't see it from the porch.

He remembered as a boy, watching his father through the months of his mother cheating on him, watching from this porch the day his mother rode away in Charlie Holmes' car, and thinking, Why doesn't he stop her? Why can't Dad stop her? And then there he was, some forty years later, he was the one leaving—the look on his wife Susan's face as he packed his suitcases and left the house, loaded up his car, the expressions of his two children, Lori and David, eight and ten, and he wouldn't look at them, wouldn't even think about them, because he knew he was going to leave regardless, regardless what anybody said, that nothing was going to stop him—and he couldn't say why.

Thirty-three

Oh, he knew well enough the occasion for his leaving his marriage. He knew the day he saw Sheryl walk in the door of the agency—the younger woman in her high heels and tight skirt, perfect legs—he knew he was going to try to fuck her. The same way he knew, as soon as he did once, that he was going to keep fucking her or try to, knew after a year or so of sneaking around that he had to either go back to the way things were or leave his wife and family and move in with Sheryl. His marriage had been as different as could be from that of his mother and father—he and Susan talked all the time, took the kids on trips to Disney World, the cabin at Seven Springs, Hawaii, watched their favorite TV shows together, went to movies, the kids' soccer and baseball games, dance lessons for heaven's sake, laughed together all the time—and yet the result was the same. Though not quite the same either: His mother ended up coming back. Since his affair with Sheryl fell apart, William lived by himself, in a townhouse in a development of his own making near South Pointe.

All this time. All those years. He blamed his father for not stopping his mother from leaving. And it took a trip back here to realize that his father couldn't have stopped her even if he had wanted to. The fact was that if William was going to blame anyone he supposed it should be his mother for the leaving. For leaving him. His foot dragged in the well-worn gouge in the floor as he swung slowly back and forth, back and forth.

Thirty-four

He thought maybe he could do some good here. Thought he could definitely help the situation. After all, he was a man of position and influence in Pittsburgh. He was sure his father couldn't afford the best care for his mother. He would find out where they were taking her—that someone was coming for her indicated a public institution of some kind—he'd pull some strings and get her admitted to the best private assisted living facility in the area, take over the financial responsibility. His father would be against it, of course, some prideful notion of taking care of her himself, but William was certain he could override any objection, use legal means if need be, he had the resources to do that, it would be for the best, for both his mother and his father, in the long run. Then he could tackle the problems of the farm itself, what to do with the old man. His father surely couldn't expect to keep working the place, he was in his eighties, for that matter he shouldn't be driving on the highway at this point either, that was another thing William needed to look into; he needed to make sure the value of the place was secure, that the paperwork was in order for easy transfer if his father was declared non compos mentis—before his actual passing—that is, if the old man wasn't gone in the head already, keeping his mother here on the farm this long was certainly questionable. The thought of what he could do here to set things right filled him with a sense of accomplishment, a satisfaction that he could make a difference. . . .

The tractor was on him before he realized it was this close to the house. His father drove the machine across the barnyard, the empty spreader bouncing along behind, to beside the barn and backed the spreader in position under the hopper of the manure trolley. He climbed down from the tractor—William noted how stiffly the man moved, half bent over with arthritis; yes, the old man couldn't expect to work much longer in this condition— unhitched the spreader, climbed back up behind the wheel of the tractor—William winced in sympathy with the pain his father must be feeling—then drove the tractor across the yard to the disc harrow sitting in the grass near the equipment barn, repeated getting down from the tractor, hitching up the harrow, climbing up back behind the wheel, and started back across the yard the way he'd come, towing the harrow, close to the house. When he noticed William on the porch, his father looked at him, staring at him, meeting his eyes or so it seemed, his head on a slow swivel, but kept going, on toward the fields.

Thirty-five

What was his name? I can't remember now. But I remember I liked him at one time—he wasn't that nice man who comes around now to help me eat and go to the bathroom. He was that other one. No, I take it back, I don't think I ever really liked him, truth be told. But there were things about him I liked. I liked the way he smelled. And I liked his starched white shirts, not when he took off his suit coat, but when he had his suit coat on, that line of starched white cuff, maybe two inches, maybe three, between the sleeve of his jacket and his hand. The skin of his hand the color of brown shoe polish, I thought for a while he might be Spanish or something, beautiful skin, but it was only because he was outside in the lot of the dealership so much; when he took off his suit coat and shirt, his arms, his shoulders and chest under the strings of his undershirts were a different kind of white, pale as a slug exposed under a log, his hands looking like gloves at the end of white sticks.

I'll say this about the nice man, he always wore T-shirts under his work clothes. He always stayed covered up.

Thirty-six

I liked that other one because for once I felt I had a choice, that I could make a choice on my own, that I wasn't simply following something that was preordained, the result of some greater force from on high or from deep within, that I could decide for myself. Though choice is a slippery thing, isn't it, it can slip right through your fingers and wrap itself around you, tie you up hand and foot, even stick a gag in your mouth, before you know it. And I did like the other one's hands, the long slender fingers, Noah's fingers—that's right, that's what the nice man's name is, now I remember—his fingers were stubby and always bunged up, with cuts and tears, the dirt ground into the whorls of his skin as if he were always inked for fingerprints, always a suspect. The other one's hands were delicate, fingers like a pianist, I guess I thought it meant he must be sensitive, that he'd be considerate. But he was the same as all the others, he kept coming at me. Wanting me. I never wanted to be wanted. But that's not true either. I wanted to be wanted without the wanting. It took me a while to learn there's a difference between the wanting and what is wanted. . . .

Thirty-seven

Towing the disc harrow behind the tractor, Noah retraced his route across the newly manured field, slicing the ground and mixing the manure with the soil, along with chopping up the weeds and remains of the crops from the last time he planted this section, making it easier to plow later when he was ready to plant again. Remembering that it was William who showed him where Maddie was living after she moved out. After she moved in with Charlie Holmes. One day a few weeks after she left she picked up the boy from where the bus dropped him off after school and drove him to Seneca on the other side of Furnass and showed him their fancy new townhouse. William told his father about it later that evening: his mother told William that he could come visit them anytime he liked, gave him a phone number to call and said she would come out to the farm and get him.

"Did she offer to let you move in with them?" Noah said, washing their dinner dishes in the sink.

"No," the boy said, sitting at the table, tracing the outlines of the red and white squares on the plastic tablecloth.

"Because if you wanted to, I could ask her for you."

"Why would you do that? Are you trying to get rid of me?"

Noah turned and looked at him. "I thought maybe the school in Seneca was better than Furnass. That it might prepare you better for going to college."

"No. Seneca is actually worse. There's a lot of drugs and stuff. The rich kids from there and Highland Hills have enough money to pay for them."

"Well, when you want to go in for a visit, let me know and I can take you. And pick you up, if she doesn't want to bring you out again."

"Why would you do that? Why would you want to make it easier for her?"

They looked at each other for a moment, then the boy got up from the table and went into his room. Noah turned back to the dishes. He didn't have an answer to that—yes, why would he want to help her, after what she had done to the family? After what she had done to him? Thinking back as he bumped along on the tractor, churning up the field behind him, he had no more of an answer now than he did then. He did know, however, that without meaning to—in doing what he knew he needed to do for Maddie's sake, what he knew she needed from him, what he needed to do if he was ever going to get her back again—in William's eyes he had let the boy down. Again.

Thirty-eight

As Noah stopped the tractor beside the equipment barn, turned off the engine, and climbed down from the cab—stiffly, choosing where he stepped carefully, keeping a grip on the handhold so he didn't slip, the last step down sending a shooting pain from his ankle to thigh and beyond—William was already off the porch and coming toward him. The expression on his face that of a man set to make things right.

"You saw your mother?" Noah said, trying to mask his limp, slipping back the collar on the power take-off, disengaging it from the tractor.

"Yes, I saw her. Nobody's come for her yet. Is there something we should be doing to get her ready? I mean, is she packed? I didn't see any suitcases. . . ."

"She's not going anywhere. Nobody's coming for her. She's staying right here."

He could imagine the befuddlement on his son's face but he didn't look at him. He busied himself unwinding the turnbuckles on the stabilizer shafts, removing the linchpins on the link arms.

"What are you talking about?" William said after a moment. "The doctor's office said—"

"The doctor's office made some assumptions. Before they talked to me. Before they found out what I intend to do. I'm keeping her here on the farm. Where she belongs."

He tried reaching across and pushing the right link arm, to move it off the pin, but he couldn't get the leverage. Finally, he braced himself and kicked at it with the bottom of his boot. That did it. . . .

Thirty-nine

"But how will you take care of her? You can barely get around yourself."

"You're the one standing here. I'm the one unhitching a harrow. You want to rethink that?"

"You know very well what I mean. You'll need help, how will you pay—"

"I told you. I'll still be raising beef cattle." With the link arms free, he reset the linchpins, then took a rag from his back pocket and wiped his hands, wiped his forehead. "That will give me more time around the house to help her through the day. And I've lined up people from church to stop by now and then. And when she needs medical help, I can pay for that too. I didn't tell you, I sold the gas rights. They're putting in at least one well here, maybe two. Start next week."

"You can't do that."

"Afraid I already have. I'm sorry if those gas wells spoil your plans for subdividing the place."

Noah folded the kerchief and put it back in the rear pocket of his overalls. Then looked up at his son. He wants to hit me, Noah thought. Or cry. He not only lost his mother today, once and for all, but lost this place too. A lot of dreams shot to hell. He figures he lost me years ago so I don't count.

William turned and walked away, back across the yard, got in his car and drove away.

Forty

The midnight blue Audi fishtailed in the loose gravel at the end of the drive, the stones pinging up against the undercarriage, dust flying, as William, knowing he was going faster than he should, swung out onto the road, into the path of a neighbor's tractor towing a hay wagon. William fought for control of the car, careened onto the narrow shoulder, missing the front of the tractor by inches, the tall grass from the field beside the car whipping into his open windows, and back onto the asphalt again, on down the narrow road toward Furnass, back to the freeway headed north that would take him home to Pittsburgh.

Thinking, That's it. He had had it. He had tried to help his parents, now that they were in their closing years, tried to mend the broken bridges between them, and this is what he got for it. His offer of help thrown back in his face. It was exactly what he couldn't stand, it was precisely what he had tried to get away from his whole life: the backwoods, farm-bred, countrified way of thinking, the suspicion of any new idea, or for that matter anybody else's idea rather than your own, anything that would let anyone else into their lives, anything that might help make their lives better, such as letting their well-to-do successful son help with their healthcare expenses—heaven forbid! That much-vaunted America-in-the-heartland self-reliance that was just another way of saying they were conservative to the core and basically too uneducated and uninformed—and face it: basically unintelligent—afraid of the bigger, wider outside world, thinking they could do everything themselves, without asking advice or counsel, even from their own son, who might know something about land deals and gas rights.

Forty-one

No, it wasn't his parents, they weren't the problem; it was his father, William's own image of American Gothic; the old fool, if his father had let William take over management of the land his parents would have more than enough to support them the rest of their lives, not only support them but allow them to live comfortably for once, but no, now his father had ruined it for all of them, and why, because the old man was sure he knew best—the farmer as custodian of the earth, he who giveth and he who taketh away, dispenser of life and death—now he had condemned his wife to a death-in-life of second-rate healthcare and hardscrabble facilities until there was nothing left of her, until she withered away like the folds of her wrinkled mind and his father could sit back and take satisfaction in the knowledge that he had done it all on his own, created a hell of his own devising, world without end. . . .

Forty-two

He remembered when he was six or seven, he couldn't have been much older than that because his mother hadn't left yet, one of the cows dropped a calf in the pasture, and even from the house William could tell something was wrong; when it finally tried to stand one hind leg was limp, a three-legged calf, and his father who had been there through the birth drove away on the tractor as the mother licked the baby clean and returned towing the cart and William thought, My dad is going to help it, take it to the vet or something, he'll make it right; but his father, after herding the mother up the hill to the rest of the cows, came back to the calf, took his rifle from the cart, and shot the calf between the eyes, dropped it where it stood, then wrestled the body into the bed of the cart, drove back behind the barn and dumped the body into the pit he kept for waste and William said to himself, So that's who he is, life means nothing to him, he gives life as well as takes it away, he has no use for the weak or damaged, it's only the strong and the fit who have a chance to make it in his eyes; and thought, This man is my enemy, I have to be on guard against him if I'm going to survive because if I show weakness he might come for me too; and he thinks now: It all started there, witnessing him shoot that crippled calf, I learned to fear him and dread him and hate the farm way of thinking, the bedrock beliefs that life is cheap and expendable and only worth keeping if it's useful, if it can be made use of—that farm mindset that was okay with it when Mom decided to leave and just as non-committal when she came back again, that life is easy come, easy go—that I could be expendable too if I wasn't careful, if I didn't keep watch every moment. . . .

Forty-three

Or maybe that wasn't it at all, he thinks as he crosses under the freeway outside of Furnass, doubles back on himself as he circles up the on-ramp, maybe it was never about his father, or his mother either for that matter, the farm way of life, maybe it was his fear at that young age that he'd never measure up to a man who could look a calf in the eye and blow its brains out or of a woman who could walk away from her own child, though he needn't have worried, he knows he's proven himself more than capable of showing his own disregard for life, in business dealings, with his own wife and children, but he's secure in himself, that he's proven himself to his own standards of success and love; besides none of this seems to have any bearing on the two old people he's leaving behind on the farm, he can see no reason why he would ever come back until one or the other has died, for the obligatory funeral, and maybe not even then, circling up into the speeding traffic, racing north toward the life that awaits him in the city. . . .

Forty-four

I was driving home that night from the restaurant and traffic on the highway was stopped ahead, a few cars, and I got out to see what was going on, there was a young deer on the side of the road, it was frozen in the headlights standing next to the barrier on the edge of the concrete overpass, looking like at any second it would panic and try to jump over the side, into a canyon, it must have been a hundred feet straight down, and one of the locals brushed past me in the hurry to get back to his truck, "I got my rifle in the cab, I'm going to have me some venison," he said to the few of us standing there, and then one of the soldiers from a carload heading back to Fort Campbell walked over to the deer talking to it the whole time, I recognized the guy from the restaurant, he would always talk to me but all the soldiers talked to me, I knew what they were trying to do, at least most of them so I never paid that much attention to this one, I only knew he was a little different, he was always talking about the farm he came from in Western Pennsylvania, how pretty it was and all, and he'd always ask me how I was doing or how I was holding up in that cute Yankee accent of his, and now he was talking that way to the deer, asking it as calm as could be as if he and the deer were old friends how it was doing and that it must be pretty scared with all these lights and not knowing which way to get out of there, he stood beside the deer still talking to it and then petted it on its neck, the animal quivering for a second and we all thought that was going to make the deer jump but then the deer settled down looking at the soldier with those big brown liquid eyes as if it understood everything he was saying to it or at least that he was trying to help. . . .

Forty-five

. . . By that time the local was back with his gun and as he raised it to his shoulder he said, "Better get out of the way, soldier, unless you want shot too," I guess he was trying to make a joke out of it or something but the soldier said, in the same tone of voice, as if he was still talking to the deer, "Then you better shoot me first because if you try to shoot this deer I'm coming over there and take that weapon away from you and beat you to death with it," and the local laughed a little, looking around at us as if to share in the joke but none of us were laughing, especially none of the other soldiers with the one petting the deer, and before anything else could happen the soldier, his hand on the deer's neck, started walking it along the barrier, still talking to it like an old friend, guiding it along, directing it, walked it all the way to the end of the overpass and then patted it once more to get it going and to tell it it was safe now and the deer took off down the embankment of the highway and into the dark woods beyond, and all of us standing there in front of our cars applauded except the local with the gun who muttered something and the young soldier turned and looked at him and finally the local went back to his truck and I knew at that moment I would marry that young soldier, and I remembered more of what he was always telling the other soldiers about his farm back in Western Pennsylvania, its patchwork fields and sharp little hills and the woods changing from green to reds and oranges and yellows and then

· *333* ·

appearing lifeless all winter long only to burst into green again to mark the seasons and the highway that ran right through the middle of the place and I knew that I'd go there with him some-day and see it for myself, that once and for all I'd feel safe and cared for no matter what I did, even if I did everything possible to mess it up, because I knew he'd come after me when it was time like he did the frightened deer but that was so long ago even though it seems like it happened just a few minutes ago, I can't understand why he doesn't come for me now, something's happened to me and I don't know what it is, how did I ever get like this, where am I?

Forty-six

She had been gone two years almost to the day—almost as if she planned it that way though he didn't think she did, though if she hadn't been keeping track he had—when she called late one morning when she knew he'd be through milking and said without saying who it was, knowing she didn't need to, "I want to come home," and he said, "Are you at that townhouse?" and she said, "Yes," and he said, "Is he there?" and she said, "No, but he could be at any time, I guess you should be ready," and he didn't say anything, he didn't need to, they both knew he would be ready enough, he had been waiting to be ready since she left, and with William at school Noah drove to the townhouse complex in Seneca and pulled his pickup into the driveway of #313 behind Charlie's silver convertible, the engine ticking cool as Noah walked up the flagstones to the front door, not bothering to knock, ready to bust it off its hinges if by chance it was locked, and found the two of them in the front hall, Maddie's collection of luggage and several additional cardboard boxes stacked around her like a little fort, Charlie standing in front of her, his hands open like a man ready to catch a baby dropped from the upper floor of a burning building, saying to her, "Why? You at least owe me that."

Noah looked at him, looked at her to make sure he was reading things correctly, and said, calmly, in that regular voice he used once to talk to the deer ready to jump off the overpass and to the redneck local who threatened to shoot him, "She don't owe you a thing. You owe her for not asking me to break your neck."

Charlie raised back into himself with plump indignation. "What gives you the right to walk in here and threaten me and take away a woman who is wearing the clothes I bought her and has been eating my food and living in my house for the past two years?"

Noah couldn't help but smile. "Seeing as how we're talking about my wife, you might want to rethink the what-gives-you-the-right argument."

Forty-seven

About this time it must have occurred to Charlie that Noah's smile had a bite to it, like a wolf or bear about to attack might be thought to smile because its teeth were showing. "Well, at least we can be civil about this. Here, let me give you a hand with some of these boxes."

When they were away from the townhouse, they rode in silence through the suburbs and into the farmland beyond, the windy country roads that led back toward the farm. She spoke only once, and that was as they passed the fields exploding with wildflowers, fields of mustard seed, on the way to the house. "Did you plant oats this year?"

"No," he said. "Timothy."

Forty-eight

They never talked about her time away, they never discussed the reasons, neither one finding it necessary. When William got home that day, he found his mother in the kitchen making dinner. He didn't say anything either, until a few days later when Noah was working on the engine of the tractor and looked up to see William in the doorway, looking at him. Noah finished wire-brushing the spark plug in his hand, then checked the gap, bending the outside of the electrode to the specified .030, giving the boy time.

"So. Is Mom home for good now?"

Noah fit the plug back in the engine block, tightening it with the socket wrench. He straightened up and looked at the boy, wiping his hands on a rag before answering. "Yes."

"What made her come back?"

"Nothing made her, unless it was something inside her. She was just ready to."

"Is she going to go away again?"

"No. I don't 'spect so." He leaned back into the engine, fitted the wire on the plug, then took the socket wrench and switched the direction of the ratchet and began to loosen the next one in line. "Are you glad she's back?" he asked over his shoulder.

"Yeah. Of course. But it never had anything to do with me, did it?"

"No, I guess it didn't."

"That's too bad." William stood there a moment longer, then walked away. Noah watched him in the frame of the doorway as if in a picture, the small figure making his way across the barnyard, kicking at a couple of the barn cats in his way, then out across the fields, his blue jeans and white T-shirt lost soon enough in the tall grass.

Forty-nine

Noah sat on the tractor parked beside the equipment barn. At the time he had the talk with William, a few days after the boy's mother came back to the farm, Noah didn't understand what the boy meant. But he thought he did now. William knew even then that he was an afterthought—no, that wasn't the right word; but the boy knew he wasn't the main thought. He was a by-product, conceived in love—or what was called making love—but his arrival was no more intended or intentioned than the blossoming of a field of wildflowers. A flourishing of nature, a natural act, the multiplying and division of cells, buds breaking through the soil looking for sunlight, tendrils reaching into the earth for darkness. It had always been about Noah and Maddie, the love if that was what you called it—her need for him to take care of her, his need to take care of.

He guessed that was what his life amounted to, what it was about: taking care of things. It wasn't so much that he was good at it, he didn't know if that was true or not, but it was all he knew, all that he knew to do. With William, even as a baby, it was obvious that, beyond the essentials of food and clothing, shelter and safety, the boy could take care of himself—or recognized that he'd have to. He didn't want or need to be taken care of, the one thing of his own that Noah could give to him, the only thing he knew how to give. Take care of him in the same way that he would have taken care of a field that needed tending, a cow that needed fed or watered, milked. Caring for, his only way of caring. It was as far as his feeling of affections could go, for any person, because his deepest feelings, whatever he might wish to feel, were reserved for Maddie, because Maddie's need for caring for was deeper, stronger. Maybe it wasn't love between them, but it was what they knew, what they shared.

Fifty

Now sunlight and shadow chased each other across the hills, the fields, as the clouds streamed out of the west, moving in fast, driven by an approaching cold front, the rain from the Great Plains and the Midwest heading east, the movement of the planet in its daily round, the lowering of the sunlight at the end of the day setting the late afternoon in deep relief. Sitting on the tractor looking at the scene, the hills and fields and woods he knew so well, that were part of him, he was happy, or what he knew of happiness, content, taken by the beauty of the land and of the day, all he knew or ever wanted to know. He brushed a couple flies away, attracted to the sweat on his face, said out loud, "Come on, old son, let's get on with it. The girls are waiting." He'd do the milking, the few cows that remained, then get to the house. See what Maddie might need.

AFTERWORD

BRIAN TAYLOR

The soul never thinks without an image.

Aristotle

As we soon realize when using a camera and a pen, photography and writing are each challenge enough for a lifetime of exploration and expression. In this poetic and powerful collection of photographs and short stories, Richard Snodgrass reveals his mastery of these two forms of "telling." Both image and text are narratives, yet neither yields nor explains the other; the photographs are not illustrations just as the words are not captions. Each remains independent, as siblings in the same family might tell a story from different vantage points, or the way lyrics intertwine with musical notes to create a song larger than the sum of its parts.

Each story is introduced by a single photograph, gravity-bound in its silent, wordless existence. The scenes portrayed are imbued with a heaviness, laden with the weight of human life and time— time before, during and after the lives of the characters who live and work upon its soil. Lives that will someday be lowered into the earth, joined and forever one with the land. The pictures are beautifully composed, containing subtle textures and intricate tonalities mirroring the shading of the lives described in the stories. The somber earth tones of the photographs are the perfect monochromatic color to represent the measure of hope in the characters' lives— not resplendent or radiantly colored with opportunity. At times, the images feel like open windows that could be viewed and contemplated by the characters in the stories, carrying and recalling memories from their lives.

The text is visual as well, presenting the wrinkled skin under tired eyes, the folded handkerchief in a farmer's back pocket, the dirt under fingernails, the patting of a small boy's head against his will, the eyes of husbands & wives meeting, then quietly looking away. Richly layered with life's unfolding events, the stories also capture the spaces in between events, words, and conversations. These are the life-changing pauses, quiet and imperceptible, containing unspoken understandings and misunderstandings that profoundly influence and set in motion the remaining course of a lifetime. Snodgrass is a master of such quiet awareness, exploring the silent, liminal spaces between us, moments of waiting, pause and contemplation. As in the beautifully piercing moment of realization in the space within two men's conversation, "... about this time it must have occurred to Charlie that a smile had a bite to it, like a wolf or a bear about to attack might be thought to smile because it's teeth were showing." Or capturing a stunned father's silent, uncertain thoughts after his son tells him, "Seems to me you always let a lot of things slip through your fingers."

These short stories reveal the diaphanous interactions between family, friends and neighbors through their challenges of daily existence in this fictional small town of Furnass, PA. These are stories about work and romance, yearning and hope, sadness and endurance, coping and escaping, forbidden yet often consummated temptations. The characters are often restless in their lives, yet lack the awareness or opportunity to change their plight. At times we enter into lives and conversations in an exhilarating midstream journey. We witness the introspection of the characters looking backwards in time and then forward, trying to make sense of an unyielding, often merciless world. There are the somber realizations of a young wife seeing her life laid out before her, knowing that: "... her marriage was never going to be different. That they were going to be just like everybody else." We are witness to people trapped in the stillness of their rooms:

"the house settled around her like a familiar shawl." These are moments of quiet resignation we can all relate to: "We are watching our lives play out in front of us." And later: "... thinking, so this is how it happens. This is when you start to know."

In stories that unfold indoors, the words and pictures become still lifes of still lives. Snodgrass intricately records the characters' homes in a powerful documentary style. The photographs are intimate collections of sweaters, bed sheets, pillboxes, recliners, windows and drapes— the actual fabric of people's lives. These interiors are biographies in plain sight, containing the confessional patina of our valued objects. Snodgrass astutely realizes that still photographs can actually show the passage of time in quiet depictions of teetering piles of newspapers and magazines that reached their heights by slowly rising over weeks, months and years. In a conversation with the author, Snodgrass explained: "If you really want to know somebody, look at the things they think are important and surround themselves with. The things really tell you who they are, what they value. And are immutable testaments of the life they live."

All of life's lessons are here clear and sharp as a surgeon's knife, the inhalations and realizations between our words and actions. The power of these stories arises from our uneasy recognition that such moments inhabit every day of our own waking lives. In the end, Snodgrass offers us a universality in the fates of these isolated characters, revealing the temptations and possibilities we recognize in our own lives, inviting us to consider the consequences of the yearnings and desires we carry with us on our own journey. And for these considerations let us lead better lives, through a greater awareness of: "the movement of the planet in its daily round, the lowering of the sunlight at the end of the day setting the late afternoon in deep relief."

ACKNOWLEDGMENTS

There are four people—friends, actually; dream catchers—without whom I could never have brought these books to publication:

Kim Francis
Bob Gelston
Dave Meek
Jack Ritchie

I also thank Eileen Chetti for struggling through my quirks of style and punctuation. I particularly thank Jack Ritchie who took on the task of designing the covers so I wouldn't, in his words, embarrass myself, and who has long served as a sounding board, bullshit detector, and all-round good friend. And then, of course, there's my wife Marty. . . .

The photographs in this book were all taken between 2005 and 2012 near Hickory, PA. In addition to Chip, Jo Ann, and Adam Cowden—who were the first I approached to photograph their farm, and whose graciousness, kindness, and support was and is beyond words—I also wish to thank the late Bill Dinsmore, the late Nello and Norma Mungai, Guy Cowden, Mike Wussick, Tom Davis, and the late Marge Caldwell Curran for access to their respective farms.

Line drawings are by an itinerate and largely overlooked painter named Emil Bott, from an original copy of *Caldwell's Illustrated Historical Centennial Atlas of Washington County, PA*, 1876.

Richard Snodgrass lives in Pittsburgh, PA with his wife Marty and two indomitable female tuxedo cats, raised from feral kittens, named Frankie and Becca.

Brian Taylor was born in Tucson, Arizona. He received his B.A. Degree in Visual Arts from the University of California at San Diego, an M.A. from Stanford University, and his M.F.A. from the University of New Mexico, studying with Van Deren Coke and Beaumont Newhall.

Brian taught as a Professor of Photography at California State University, San Jose for 40 years, served as the Chair of the Department of Art and Art History, and retired as a Professor Emeritus in 2017. Brian also served as the Executive Director of the Center for Photographic Art in Carmel, California from 2015-2019, retiring as Director Emeritus to return to his studio practice.

To read more about the Furnass series, the town of Furnass, and special features for *Furrow and Slice*—including author interviews, the entire series of photographs, additional line drawings, and omitted scenes—go to www.RichardSnodgrass.com.

Emil Bott, Self-Portrait, circa 1870,
Southwestern Pennsylvania